VERSION OF

BOND & BENEVOLENCE:

GOOD RAIDER

RELEASED

10/09/2014

THE FOLLOW UP:

GOOD RADICAL

11/09/2014

EBOOK/PAPERBACK

@

ALL LOCAL BOOKSTORES

&

KINDLE/B&N/ITUNES

THIS BOOK IS NOT TO BE SOLD

Delegate Publishing

The book is a work of fiction. Any references to historical events, real people or real locales are used factiously.

ISBN: 9780996075725

Artwork created by J. C Johnston & Delegate Pub.

Profile Photographer: Nick Crawford

Chapters

The Bond & Benevolence Series by J. C. Johnston is written on the premise of relinquishing the material things in this world and becoming more benevolent to others that are less fortunate. The more someone begins to care the more sacrificial and passionate that person becomes. Thus the motto:

Compassion Breeds Determination

Dedication

It is with joy that I dedicate this book to my wife Lorraine. She certainly would not want me to do so but I don't always do what she wants. She truly has taught me how to bond and be benevolent. To trust and wait for the best outcomes. I am still a work in progress. Aren't we all?

J.C Johnston

1

LETTING GO

When I was a very young child, my desires and their consequences were not too hard to live with. As I got older, things became more difficult. I only hope that what I wish for now doesn't cost too much, and I can live with the outcomes. We all hope for things without knowing what blessings or curses will come with them.

Over time, as my wishes have come true, I have found myself either cherishing the rewards so much that I worried incessantly about losing them or begging God to take them back. Yes, I rarely ever made wishes without some elaborate deal with the God of my mother to grant them. My obsession with music, the instruments that produced it, and Mamma's obsession for me, her little Ophelia, to become successful drove me to make many elaborate deals with God. By the time I was fourteen, I owed Him much more than I could ever pay Him in this life. Maybe that is why He has taken so much from me.

Why so many wishes? All my life, I had caught a glimpse of the other side of the fence. Most of the time, getting over that fence would require a helping hand that most never receive. But I was one of the lucky ones, or so I thought. Greenwich, Connecticut, where my mother worked as a maid for a wealthy stockbroker, and where she took me during my vacations from school when she could not afford a babysitter, offered a view over the social fence between the haves and have-nots. It was where I would receive my first real instrument–my first leg up in climbing from poverty and mediocrity to wealth and greatness.

Early spring yard sales in the ritzy neighborhood, where some of the richest and most famous people in the United States lived, always brought people from all walks of life. Many of the sale shoppers were people like my mother. Butlers, maids, nannies, and gardeners were the main link between two worlds. We all knew the joy it brought to find expensive things for pennies on the dollar. People traveled from five towns over to the suburbs, looking for a good deal on things we wished for; we would find these treasures camouflaged by dust and grime but in great condition, well preserved by the mild temperatures of a basement or attic. Shoes, books, handbags, clothes—everything you can imagine would find a new lease on life when they were the right fit for a yard sale customer.

Even among these fabulous, affluent suburban neighborhood sales, Mr. Raider's yard sales were renowned for having the best items. People of every race, color and creed would arrive by the carloads on a beautiful, warm summer day, excited about the treasure hunt. That was the beauty of it all–never knowing what you were going to find. The spring of 2009, Mr. Raider had collected goods from several of his neighbors to make sure he would never disappoint the crowd.

No one knew why it meant so much to him to please us. Was it to assuage his guilt for being so privileged? We didn't care. Sometimes, he would have to pry some of those goods from his daughter Samantha, who would suddenly recall the good times she had spent with these now-neglected things and refuse to part ways with them. But that year, it was different for Samantha, who was now seventeen.

Losing Hyacinth, her nanny and tutor, who had become like a mother to her after six years of care, had a profound effect on her. To honor Hyacinth's memory, Samantha now strove to live by her teacher's altruistic teachings.

On her tenth birthday, Sam was given a light pink Schwinn bike worth about as much as one of the old cars that had come for the yard sale and looked out of place on this affluent street. The Schwinn bicycle she named Bugsy became more important than all the dolls she had collected and even more important than the tree house her dad had built the year before.

Samantha loved the seaside but had been required to wait for her father to bring her when he felt like it. But with Bugsy, almost daily during summer months, she would sneak away and ride as fast as she could, carrying bread or crackers to feed the Seagulls, her hat and snacks in the basket attached to the front handlebars. Now, she saw herself as an adult. She had outgrown the bike with its girlish decorations and thick, stable frame and had picked out a faster, sleeker one.

For blocks around, everyone admired Sam as they saw her zipping by with her slender, muscular dancer's frame and her long blond hair, sometimes down over her shoulders, and sometimes wrapped tight in a dancer's bun.

Browsing at the yard sale that day was the Full Gospel Mission's pastor from Port Chester, New York, one town over from Greenwich. The pastor was collecting used bicycles all over Connecticut to ship to the small orphanages his church had founded around the world. He thought of the ten-year-old girl who had tugged on his heart strings during his recent trip to the Philippines.

This cycle would be perfect for Lele, he thought as he walked vigorously towards it. *Perfect size, perfect color, and in great condition. This bicycle was treated with love.* Samantha walked over to the tall, well-dressed pastor and started to talk to him, making sure he had good intentions for her old friend.

"My Dad is forcing me to sell this Schwinn bicycle, but I don't want to part with it," she said to the pastor. "It had some truly good days. His name is Bugsy."

The pastor smiled with warmth, his kind brown eyes meeting her blue ones, and shook his head, realizing that this bike meant a lot to her. "Well, I can promise you that Bugsy will end up in good hands. A little girl from the Philippines named Lele will become the proud owner of this bicycle if you sell it to me.

Lele will cherish and love him just as much as you did."

"Are you sure?" Samantha asked.

"Maybe you would like to check in on Bugsy every now and then," the pastor answered. "Why don't you become pen pals with Lele? That way you can find out everything you need to know about Bugsy."

"I would like that very much," Samantha answered excitedly.

And so, Sam wrote the pastor's information in her little book. Feeling good about the new owner to be, Sam felt much better about relinquishing Bugsy.

This was the eleventh bicycle the pastor had bought. Soon they would be ready for the six week trip across the Pacific Ocean. All the other bikes needed refurbishing, but not Samantha's. After a month sitting in a warehouse behind the church, Bugsy's new adventure began.

As the yard sale continued, it was evident that Sam and Mr. Raider had found that giving away their things was just as fulfilling as making a little spending change. It's not like they needed the money. The good feeling brought them together.

For Samantha and others, the yard sale had become a great way to make new friends. Most of the attendees would not otherwise have had this sort of contact. The yard sales brought together neighbors who had not spoken for years, and inner-city dwellers with suburbanites whom they might not have spoken to at all without this pretext. One such relationship was sparked when a young woman from Africa named Ofi tried to buy a big pot that had been Hyacinth's favorite pot to cook stew in. One look at the pot's beautiful floral decorations and Ofi knew what it would mean to her family, but a woman who had come with the pastor had already purchased it. A sticker on it read "sold."

Ofi walked up to the woman and struck up a conversation.

"Hello. Getting good deals here?" Ofi asked the lady.

"I am, actually," she answered. "I'm Sherri."

"I'm Ofi. Very pleased to meet you."

"I've been coming to Mr. Raider's yard sale for several years now from two towns over," Sherri said as she smiled ear to ear. "I have never been let down. You guys are not from here either are you?"

"No way," Ofi answered. "We came to get some good deals on goods to bring back to our family in Darfur. I go every six months. We have been saving our tax refund for these yard sales."

The conversation continued, and soon Sherri also wanted Ofi's family to have the pot. Sherri was a Black American woman who considered Africa her homeland, though she had never been there. Sherri had bought the pot for one dollar and now gave it to Ofi for free.

Sam, who stood by watching the exchange between the two, walked over to Ofi and Sherri. After a great conversation about Hyacinth's delicious beef stew and Ofi's mother's cooking, Sam exchanged numbers with Ofi, hoping to give her more things from other neighbors for her to take to Darfur.

When Ofi arrived home that day, she placed the pot in a large suitcase with the rest of the things she would bring to Darfur on her next trip. The next day Sam called her back to Greenwich to pick up more donated goods Sam had collected from the neighborhood.

After Ofi left the yard sale, Samantha turned her attention to the two other items that she cared about–a couch that had belonged to Samantha's grandmother and a vintage violin she had received as a gift from her father when she was six years old. The couch, with cushions fit for a king, was as comfortable as they came and had served Samantha's grandmother for over twelve years.

Samantha had the couch placed in the attic, where she would recline on it during winter months and read, or stare outside the window while listening to music.

When another sale-picker, Elsie, sat in the couch, she knew it would make a great addition to the assisted-living lounge where she worked. She walked over to Samantha to make a deal.

Although she was trying, it soon became obvious that Samantha had a change of heart about parting with the couch. When asked the price of the chair, Samantha answered, "One hundred dollars."

"You have no intentions of selling this couch do you?" Elsie said and gave a friendly laugh. "Listen, whatever your connection to this couch is, I can promise you, I will bring it to some really good people who will take good care of it."

Elsie had a warmth to her that Samantha immediately felt.

"Where will you put it?" Sam asked.

"At Mount Vernon Assisted Living in New York," Elsie added. "The couch in their lobby is terrible. The springs are about to burst through."

"Well, if you promise to pay special attention to it for me and always let me know where it is, you can take it for free" Samantha said. "My grandmother truly loved that couch. The stories that she told me while sitting in that couch have stayed with me throughout the years."

"Oh my. Of course. And you are welcome to stop by and check on it."

Samantha had already decided to do her own personal little hunt to see where her favorite items would end up. After the deal was made, Samantha made her way around the yard sale looking for the violin. Samantha loved the old violin, but she hadn't used it since she turned most of her attention to dancing seven years ago. The violin was right in front of her father, who stood at a table with the more expensive goods. She opened the case it was in.

Suddenly, a cascade of memories of playing the violin overtook her. Samantha remembered her first recital and her mother's pride at her performance. She remembered when everyone in the school orchestra played together at the music hall in town. Samantha had gotten hooked on the adrenaline that came with performing, and soon she was present at every talent show her town hosted. That love for performing, though, had been transferred to dance.

Now Samantha had enrolled in the world-renowned Julliard School of Arts in New York City and was on her way to becoming a professional dancer.

While she stood there reminiscing about the violin, a twelve-year-old girl walked up to Samantha and inquired about the violin. She had light brown skin, and her hair was in sweet little braids. She was dressed as if for church.

That girl was me. I introduced myself to Samantha.

"I have always wanted to play the violin, but we could never afford to buy one," I said.

"Well this one is very expensive," Samantha answered. "You aren't here alone, are you?"

"No, my mother works over there," I answered, pointing on the other side of the rows of tables filled with goods. "I want to learn how to play so bad, but Mamma can't afford the lessons or the violin."

"Well maybe we can arrange something with your mother," Samantha replied. "I have this new idea to keep track of my favorite things to see where they end up years from now. If you promise me you will keep contact, I will allow you to take the violin home for free."

I took off running towards my mother, yelling "Mamma" across the front lawn until I got to her. I told her of Samantha's proposal, making sure to let her know that I would end up with the violin for free. My mother grew just as excited as I was and allowed me to drag her across towards Samantha. I repeated everything Samantha had told me.

"All she wants in return, Mamma, is to keep track of where the violin ends up."

"Are you sure about this?" Mamma asked with her perfect English flavored with the Spanish accent of the Dominican Republic. "Because we truly can't afford to buy this. I will gladly keep in touch and find a way to get her lessons."

"The violin's name is Charlie, short for Charles Jean Horner, the maker of the violin," Samantha said. "You take good care of it, Ophelia, and if you join your school orchestra, there will probably be a good music teacher there to teach you how to play."

Samantha took one last look at the violin, handed it to me, and started to tell me some of its intricate details and history. I listened carefully, loving every minute of our conversation. She told me I would fall in love with the violin and crave to master the instrument. It happened just as she said it would.

Our love for music had transcended our different backgrounds and created a bond that would last over time. A bond was formed between Samantha and me. That same day, Sam decided she wanted to help me fulfill my dreams of becoming a great musician and promised she would tutor me.

2

New Life

The yard sale was a great success. It had brought new meaning to sharing for Samantha and started her down a road she would've never imagined traveling. The next morning, Samantha called Mamma and arranged a 5:00 p.m. lesson. Samantha, who have never before taken public transportation, insisted on taking the train to the Bronx to give Ophelia's lesson.

Mr. Raider agreed but with the condition that he would accompany Sam to make sure she arrived safely. This was a step in the right direction for Mr. Raider, who had become overprotective and obsessed about Sam's safety ever since her mother had been brutally murdered in a home invasion and the two of them had found her body.

Mr. Raider had done his best to give Sam a new life, and had even changed their name from La Roche to Samantha's mother's maiden name to honor her. But while Sam got a new life out of the big city, Mr. Raider never seemed able to restart his.

Sam never blamed her father for his reclusive behavior and did what he wanted most of the time, but she resented his fear-driven lifestyle. Only once had her father ventured outside of their suburban neighborhood to New York City after they had moved to Greenwich. It was when Samantha's caretaker, Hyacinth, had died and they had attended her funeral at her church in the Bronx.

When Sam came crying to her about never being able to explore the world outside of Greenwich,

Hyacinth would say in her thick Jamaican accent, "The only thing you should fear in this world is God, but you need to be patient and mind your father. The life we live is guided by our experience. Most people aren't afraid of dogs until they get their rumps bitten off."

Sam wouldn't fully understand Hyacinth's statement until she found out the truth about her mother's death. Although she remained a good daughter through hard times, Sam made it clear she was now her own woman not long after she turned seventeen. Sam was ready for the world, ready for whatever fate had to throw at her. Hyacinth had prepared her well.

The dark-skinned, devout evangelical Christian woman had left quite an impression on Samantha. Samantha had become wiser than the other children, but had also taken on a rather strict moral code. A teacher back on her home island, Hyacinth, was able to teach Samantha things that children twice her age normally learned.

They spent hours talking about the importance of education and what it means to be a good person. Samantha picked up a lot of Hyacinth's mannerisms and soon, everyone noticed that Samantha had become, in some ways, a mini-Hyacinth. But most of all what stuck with Sam was Hyacinth's carefree attitude about most of the things people burdened themselves with in their lives.

"We have little control over this world or our lives," Hyacinth told Mr. Raider after he refused to let Sam go to her high school prom unless he was there every step of the way. "The minute we try to exert control is when the powers that be will show us we have none."

When Hyacinth died, Samantha lost her best friend. She became quiet and withdrawn for most of her final year in high school. She thought about her mother more and spent most of her time in the attic where her mother's old stuff had been stored. Samantha had rummaged through everything, trying to find new traces of her mother's past life.

Caroline Raider had been a very successful ballerina when she shocked New York City by giving up dancing to raise Sam. In the Raider's giant home were photos of her with other famous New Yorkers, fabulous dresses, and even a coveted Emmy encased in a protective frame. But seeing that stuff was bittersweet for Samantha. She realized that her mother was a socialite who loved and was adored by everyone around her, nothing like the lonely suburbanite Sam was becoming.

Sam remembered how badly she wanted to be like her mother and still did. Her mother's friends were designers, artists and Broadway directors who blazed through New York City, lighting a fire over their names for everyone to see. Sam, by contrast, had been more focused on *things.*

Sheltered by her father and content with Hyacinth as a companion, the closest to friends were the material possessions she had now sold and given away. Her things were off to build new relationships and now, it was time for her to do the same, time to step out into the world and make a name for herself just like her mother did.

This is how Sam came to the decision that she should return to the city, where she had been born and where her mother had become a star. Traveling back to New York to interview at Julliard had proved as refreshing as she had hoped–so many people and places to see, a city with no negatives for her. She was determined to establish for herself, the love for people, and the sense of adventure her mother had claimed in NYC.

Putting herself "in the midst of it all" would be quite a challenge for a girl who had spent most of her time in her house in the suburbs only riding her bike and venturing out to the beach by herself. She was going to have to get comfortable with crowds, because her new school, Julliard, was in the middle of New York City.

3

MY GIFT REALIZED

The next day flew quickly as Sam spent the entire morning dancing at a local studio. When Sam arrived home, she threw herself in her bed and fell into a deep sleep. Her father awakened her in the afternoon by poking her shoulder. Just like always when Sam was traveling outside of Greenwich, her father demanded to accompany her. She relented because she knew her going to Julliard was going to be a shock to his system.

A trip from the lush grass and oak trees of the suburbs to the concrete of the city was enough to make Mr. Raider fidgety, but he knew he had agreed to let Sam teach me. The thirty minute train ride from Greenwich to the South Bronx was mostly frequented by workers who served the rich.

Almost half of the citizens of Greenwich traveled frequently to NYC for business or fun, but most of them bypassed the South Bronx for the more civilized Manhattan. Once they arrived into the Bronx, they would have to walk five minutes into my neighborhood, which became the main concern of her father. Hyacinth had been her caretaker and closest friend, so Sam felt comfortable walking through the predominantly Black and Latino neighborhood. That was not the case for her father whose eyes shifted back and forth as he walked faster than normal.

Cool and collected, Sam believed Hyacinth had prepared her to love and be loved by all in this world. It wasn't long that she arrived in the courtyard of the six buildings that formed a pentagon, dragging Mr. Raider along behind her. In front of the building, a group of young men stood there, almost blocking the door. Samantha felt her father's hand tighten around hers.

"It's okay, Dad," Samantha whispered as she smiled at the men. "What's up?" Samantha said to the men as she walked by, holding her head up high while she spoke. In a unified voice, five adolescent males answered her back.

"What's up, White Girl?"

"Nothing, jus' chillin'," Samantha answered as she walked into the building. I knew Sam and Mr. Raider had arrived when Mamma went running down the steps like she had seen a ghost. We knew how treacherous it was for outsiders to come to our neighborhood. Two weeks before, we had watched from our window in horror as the Chinese delivery man was beaten and robbed.

"Come, come," she beckoned as Mr. Raider hurried towards us.

"What did you say to them?" Mamma asked as they closed the door behind them.

"I just smiled and said 'What's up.'"

"Well that's all you need sometimes," Mamma answered. "Those boys can smell fear like animals in the jungle."

"Then how come they didn't maul Daddy?" Sam said as she giggled.

We all laughed as we made our way up three flights of stairs to a front door left wide open, but deep down Mamma and I sympathized with Mr. Raider.

"Ready to work?" Samantha said as she saw the violin sitting on the dinner table.

"You don't even know! I want to learn so badly," I said, smiling at Samantha.

Mr. Raider formally introduced himself to Mamma while Samantha made her way over and sat close beside me at the table. Samantha pulled out her iPad and placed it on the table. She pressed play and summoned me to listen.

"This is undoubtedly the most famous composers of all time and this is Mozart's Violin Concerto No.3. Can I borrow the violin, Ophelia?"

"This is beautiful. Are you that good?" I asked. "Are you going to play along to that?"

"I will try," Sam answered. Samantha started to play almost as beautifully as the recording. Overwhelmed with happiness, I found it hard to sit as I watched every stroke Samantha made. My eyes lit up, making Mamma happier than she had been in all of the past year. The hard life that hit us after my father had left abruptly had taken its toll on both of us. We needed something or someone new to fill the void he left behind. After ten minutes listening to Samantha play, happy tears came to my eyes. I didn't know why I was crying, but the beautiful sounds, most of which I heard for the first time, and the thought of being able to play like Samantha, soon became overwhelming.

Samantha finally stopped playing and turned off the music. It was time to teach me. Just like her world-renowned teacher had with her, she started to tell me about the history of classical music and the history behind the violin. While Samantha and I talked, Mamma and Mr. Raider sat in the living room and discussed their lives. They had experienced being single parents in a different fashion, but they had a lot in common, much more than they would have imagined. Mr. Raider was very wealthy, so he could afford to hire Hyacinth and occupy Samantha's mind with different activities and gifts.

Yet, he knew he was difficult to live with and overprotective. Even though her mother was not around, Mamma had to struggle just to put food on the table and worked so much she hardly ever had time for me. I struggled, being stuck in the apartment as Mamma would never allow me to go outside with all the gang activity, drug dealing and shootings that took place at the Pentagon Apartments. So, both Mr. Raider and Mamma felt bad about how the departure of their spouses had affected their children and forced them to become restrictive parents.

My father had become well-known around the neighborhood and would bring me to play outside with my friends in the daytime without fearing something would happen to us. Everyone respected my father because he was the neighborhood barber whom almost all the boys had visited one time or another. That didn't matter when he decided to have an affair with the Pentagon drug kingpin's wife. My father discovered he had a choice to make–leave town or face a sure death. The kingpin wasn't the only one who wanted revenge for my father's indiscretions. It was terrifying to watch my mother swinging a metal baseball bat at my father's head. I loved my father dearly, so after he left, my life deteriorated. Lackluster effort in school and a lonely home life soon led to depression and bad grades. But as I began to learn about the violin, my depression melted away and my zest for life returned.

After an hour, Mamma got up from her conversation with Mr. Raider and started to cook a home-style dinner for her guests. Samantha and I had finally reached the point where I was being taught how to hold the bow and violin the proper way. I stood up and placed the violin on my clavicle underneath my chin and tried to play. The first few sounds that I made didn't sound as beautiful as Samantha's, but they were my sounds, and I was proud of them. Mamma kept running from the kitchen to watch me make my first screeches with the violin.

"Come, help me chop up these *Yucca* yams, Mr. Raider." Mr. Raider had started to use his phone to conduct a search of the history and culture of the Dominican Republic. Mr. Raider walked quickly to the kitchen. He had enjoyed Mamma's company, and he wanted more. Mamma cooked rice, beans, *Yucca* yams, and chicken *fricassee.* The visiting Raiders had never smelled the seasoning Mamma put with the chicken, potatoes, and bell peppers.

Soon, I was able to put three notes together into the beginnings of a melody. When it was time to eat, Mamma had to pry the violin away from me. We all sat, ate, and for the first time in a long while, things seemed alright for everyone at the table. Mr. Raider commented several times on how flavorful the food was. It was evident that Sam's good gesture was returning blessings already, once she saw how happy her father was. He sat eating the food and smiling at everything that Mamma said. Sam felt good about deciding to teach me. I couldn't stop smiling, too. After dinner, Mr. Raider decided it was time to return home. As comfortable as he had become, he still wanted to leave the Pentagon before it got dark.

I lamented that Samantha had to leave. I had to tell her how I felt about our time together. Samantha promised she would return soon for another lesson. Mamma offered to walk them to the train station, but Mr. Raider rejected her offer, saying she was just a little woman who couldn't protect herself, much less a 200 pound man.

"I might be little, but don't ever underestimate me."

As she spoke, I remembered Mamma pounding a woman's face into the floor of our hallway. The woman had come to our house claiming to be my father's girlfriend and demanding to speak to him. I learned that day how quickly Mamma could become irate and transform from a dignified and educated-sounding woman into a street fighter. I was not anything like my battle-hardened mother. She and my father had done as well as they could protecting me from the constant battles of the ghetto. I'm not sure if it made a difference if they did or not, because I don't ever believe that I had it in me to become a hardened kind of person. While remainaining oblivious to my surroundings, I found myself walking past school fights with circles of kids egging on the fighters, without even pausing to look. Never impressed or frightened, I was always dreaming of other things, other lifestyles, other places–like I was born in the wrong place at the wrong time.

When Sam told me she yearned to be in the city, I found it ironic. There I was, wishing and pleading with God to take me out of that hellhole, while Sam fought with her father for his blessing to be there.

As Sam and her father walked briskly back to the train station, they exchanged words about Samantha's desire to be in the city. As they approached, they could hear the 7:00 p.m. train pulling into the station. They sprinted toward the platform where people were already boarding the train. They slipped in the closing door and found seats among the white-collared commuters fleeing New York City for the suburbs.

"We always want what we can't have, Hyacinth used to say," said Samantha between deep breaths.

While their conversation had been a little heated, this concluding statement helped her father calm down as they left the South Bronx. After a few minutes of silence, Samantha turned to her father beside her. "That felt really good Dad, being there."

Mr. Raider looked back at Samantha, feeling happy with pride but also lonely at this new evidence of his little girl growing up.

"Your mother used to be just like you. The things she did always seem to revolve around helping someone else. And it always made her happy and fulfilled."

"That is exactly how I feel," Samantha answered, smiling from ear to ear at this comparison with her mother's good qualities.

"Your mom was a good woman, and I miss her badly," Mr. Raider said. "I've found it hard to consider being with anyone else since then."

"Well, Dad, you have to trust someone and try to love again." Samantha said. I'm not going to be around all the time, you know? I don't want you to be alone now that I'm going to school."

"Don't worry about me. I'll be just fine," Raider scoffed.

"Yes, I'm sure you will be," Samantha answered sarcastically, flashing a wicked grin. "I saw you with Gina. You didn't seem to mind her company, not to mention scarfing down her food."

They both sat there, thinking of the future, thinking about where they would go from there. They arrived home quickly. These two worlds were so close and yet so far apart. Twenty-five minutes to another dimension. Samantha immediately went to bed while Mr. Raider answered his cellphone. Gina was calling to make sure they arrived home safely. Samantha dozed off into a pleasant sleep. The cellphone conversation drifted from courtesy to flirtation over the next hour, leaving both of them infatuated with the idea of seeing each other again.

4

RELINK & BOND

Word spread, and soon everyone in Greenwich knew what Samantha was trying to do. It was only one day since she had made fliers and visited some of her neighbors, many of whom she had never spoken to before that day. The responding phone calls and messages in her mailbox were greeted with delight by Samantha, who began to feel this was something she was predestined to do. When she awoke one morning after her first trip to my house, there was a note stuffed under her front door.

The message was from Ms. Doyle, three houses down. Samantha knew a lot about her, though she had never met the forty-six year old fashion designer who had moved out to Greenwich from New York City after a nervous breakdown. Not one of her neighbors had been in her house or seen her for years. Her behavior was strange and did not match that of the other famous people in the neighborhood. She had become a household name after a high-end retail chains picked up her designs. These days, as her label churned out vintage items, few knew for sure if she was alive or dead in that mansion.

Sam opened the lavender envelope with Ms. Doyle's signature on the front and began to read—

"I think what you're doing is a great idea. Come have tea with me this Friday and we will discuss."

Samantha's little project had quickly exploded in size. The thought of Ms. Doyle's gigantic home made her wonder how and where she would find space for all that stuff! Nobody Sam knew had been in the Doyle residence since the departure of her husband. Ms. Doyle only regularly spoke in person to the gardeners who came once a week. According to Mr. Raider, Ms. Doyle had simply given up on people after her husband left her six years ago for her assistant. She had been close to Ms. Doyle, helping her oversee the high-society clothing boutiques she had opened in New York, Los Angeles and London. The "backstabbing bitch" had become like the daughter Ms. Doyle never had, after she spent five years mentoring her. The woman not only stole her husband but used her money and ideas to start a rival store. The treachery had put Ms. Doyle's shops out of business and now her labels could only be found in department stores.

Most people in the neighborhood thought Ms. Doyle had lost her mind. Stories flourished about her wandering around her garden worshiping her flowers in the nude. To some, she was now "Crazy Doyle." The confident script in the note did not give off the sense of an insane woman, but it did seem a little crazy to give away most of the things in one's giant house, even for a good cause. Samantha had no idea what to expect.

Around 10:00 a.m. the next Friday, Sam approached Ms. Doyle's large front gate. There was an eight-foot wall guarding the entire property, and there were two video cameras at the gate. As Samantha strode up, her newfound sense of pride battling with the intimidation factor of the property, the large metal gate swung open. Samantha made her way towards the front door. Her eyes were caught by the huge garden of flowers of all sorts. More shone through the windows of a glass house the size of a small church. Samantha stopped and turned unconsciously to take it in, dumbfounded.

Jolted by a tap on her shoulder that she didn't expect, Sam turned to see Ms. Doyle standing there looking disheveled and frail. Sam tried to speak but found herself tongue tied. The woman looked like she had not eaten in days.

"You like my garden, I see," Ms. Doyle said. "Come, let me show you my bed of prized *Heirlooms*."

Ms. Doyle turned and started to walk towards the glass house. Samantha followed but never said a word. She didn't know what to expect from someone who seemed to care about flowers more that she cared about herself.

"The thing I like about flowers is that they don't need a mate to become beautiful creatures," Ms. Doyle added.

After careful thought, Samantha responded. "But we are human beings. We all need someone. And in any case, doesn't flowers needs bees?"

Ms. Doyle turned and looked at her impassively, then turned and opened the door to what could only be described as a living masterpiece, countless varieties of roses placed strategically and blossoming to create a perfect rainbow.

"I've seen a lot of gardens and this rivals them all," Samantha exclaimed. "Stunning."

"It's the only thing I live for these days," Ms. Doyle said. And then after a pause she continued. "But I think you can help me to change that. My gardener brought me your flyer. I have been thinking about doing something like this for years, but I just didn't have the energy or care to get started. You have inspired me, and I want to support your efforts."

"Well, I can start to collect whatever you're willing to give, but I don't have anywhere to store so many things. I don't even know how to give this much stuff away. Or whom to give it to!"

"Well, I think I can help you with that," Ms. Doyle said. "Let's go inside so we can sit and talk. Do you like ginger cookies?"

"Who doesn't?!"

As they made their way through the side door of the glass house, Samantha wondered what Ms. Doyle had planned. She recognized that she had school coming up and probably wouldn't have time for anything too involved. Regardless, she was excited to hear the thoughts of this lady who claimed to be rejuvenated by just the idea of Sam's little project.

As they crossed the threshold, Sam lost her appetite. A narrow winding path was the only way before them, as the entire hall was wall to wall with expensive antiques, piled high with magazines and unopened mail. Ms. Doyle was a hoarder! The difference between coming from the gorgeous and tranquil glass room to such a cluttered and ugly interior made Samantha's mind race with uncertainty. So much dust. Eleven bedrooms of this mayhem. Doyle had seen the look of disgust on Samantha's face.

"You know, I'm mortified," she said as she led Sam down a treacherous trail of neglected treasures. "I want you to help me give away these things so I can reclaim my house and start over with a few nice pieces," Ms. Doyle said as she started to speak much faster and choppier than before. "Please don't judge me. You're the first person to come in this house in years. I grew weary of the feeling people were just trying to get something out of me and stopped letting anyone come in here to help me. There are boxes of nice things here that I have never even opened."

From the way she spoke, Samantha could tell her new acquaintance was panicking with embarrassment. Ms. Doyle was now trying frantically to make room for her to sit on a couch in what must have once been a magnificent living room. Samantha tried to put her mind at ease by switching the subject.

"Do you have any children, Ms. Doyle," Samantha asked.

"Nope, God didn't find it in his plan to bless me with any," Ms. Doyle answered. "I did want children, very much."

"Well you could've adopted, couldn't you?"

"It was something my husband never wanted," Ms. Doyle answered solemnly. Sam began to sense that her attempt at easing the mood was backfiring.

"Well your husband is not here anymore, is he?" Samantha ventured.

"Know your place, Samantha!" Ms. Doyle yelled. "I didn't bring you here to be the boss. Little girls like you always want to be the boss!"

Astonished by what had transpired, Samantha stood up and started to look for an escape. The pathways through the unopened packages and oak heirlooms seemed to narrow. In quick fury, Ms. Doyle had jumped up and begun to make her way towards the kitchen. But she soon calmed and turned back. She saw that Samantha was upset and slowly walked towards her.

"Excuse my temper," Ms. Doyle stated. "I'm just not used to being around people any longer. Come, sit down and have tea with me. I promise no more outbursts!"

Hesitantly, Samantha turned and walked back to the couch. She sat and tried to compose herself. Doyle smiled and went to the kitchen for a tray carrying tea and cookies.

Doyle poured the tea. Sam's hands trembled. She wondered what next from the mysterious Ms. Doyle. She stayed silent, fearing Ms. Doyle might fling the hot tea on her. Ms. Doyle took one sip, set down the beautiful teacup, and began to talk.

"I have six buildings in excellent locations that are not being used. They were part of the chain of boutiques I had in my prior life. I would like to open them again, but as collection centers for donations that we will then distribute to needy overseas families. I will maintain the buildings, but what I want from you is a hands-on approach regarding who we send these things to. I just don't feel comfortable around people anymore, so I cannot do this myself. Yet, I want the goods to end up in the right hands. I want my possessions to end up in the hands of people who need them and will appreciate them. And I'm sure there are other people who feel the same way, but are not willing to give their family possessions to some two-bit hustler who is going to sell them. With my reputation and resources, and your youthful spirit and energy, I think we can build a wonderful philanthropic network."

Ms. Doyle looked Sam square in the eyes. "Of course, this will require you to travel and recruit some like-minded young people to determine where the items should go. And compile information to put in the collection centers to put donors' minds at ease."

The wheels were spinning in Samantha's head. What Doyle was asking was way more than she had ever imagined herself doing, much less at seventeen years old.

"Ms. Doyle, I'm just a high school graduate getting ready to attend college for dance. I don't think I have time for something that requires so much time and effort while I am trying to establish myself as a dancer. I wouldn't even know how to start!"

Ms. Doyle looked at Samantha and stood up.

"Well, pray on it for the next few days and you will make *the right decision,*" she said forcefully. "Anything is possible in this world if you put your mind to it."

Samantha processed what Ms. Doyle said for a minute, and then waited for Ms. Doyle to continue talking. But Doyle made it clear she was done by walking to the front door and opening it. Samantha quickly said her goodbyes as she escaped out the door. Before she could turn around to say a final goodbye, Doyle had closed the large door behind her.

Samantha began to walk home when she saw her next door neighbor, a boy she had kept at a distance until recently, despite his friendly overtures towards her. He was running to her from his own front door.

"I can't believe you went into Crazy Doyle's house," Justin whispered when he was close enough to Samantha. "I swear she killed my dog two years ago."

Samantha knew that the entire community had their misconceptions about Ms. Doyle, but the thought of her killing Justin's dog was just farfetched. She started laughing as she continued walking to her door.

"You really think she killed your dog?" Samantha asked.

"Yes!" he exclaimed." The rate of his speech showed just how spooked he was by Ms. Doyle. "I think she poisoned Jazz after he kept shitting on her lawn! The only time she comes out of the house is to look at her plants, and sometimes she comes out naked and puts her hands up in front of her plants like she is praying for them."

"Well, I think your ex-girlfriend killed your dog," Samantha answered. "She wasn't happy that you pretended to have chicken pox but then showed up at your prom with another girl. I bet I would've killed your dog if you had done that to me!"

"How do you know what you would've done when you've never even had a boyfriend?"

"Everybody knew how mad she was," Samantha answered. "Just be happy she didn't poison *you*!"

Justin kept insisting it was Ms. Doyle who killed his dog, but he knew deep down that Samantha could be right. Only days before the dog died, he received an anonymous warning that he would regret what he had done. Up until that point, Justin did whatever he wanted to do without ever thinking there would be any consequences. He now understood that the things he did in life might cost him in ways he might not expect. He wanted to be a better person and, so far, had held true to his pledge to be nicer, not just to girls, but to everyone. Losing his dog had really made Justin think, but a lot of this transformation was driven by his growing friendship with Samantha.

Samantha knew that Justin was capable of both good and bad. The blonde-haired boy with movie star features who now had another year left in high school had only become a "player" three years before when his father had landed a role on a popular soap opera. Suddenly, Justin was the mean kid on the block whose parents let him get away with everything. After Justin found out that Samantha's mother was killed, he came to her window every night and tried to talk to her. She told him to go away until his dog was killed. Then she felt sorry for him, too, and eventually welcomed his visits. She saw that he really was willing to listen, not just brag like he used to do. Still, she was wary of him trying to take advantage of her like he had done to the other girls before.

Later, when the weather turned cold, Sam allowed Justin to sneak in through her bedroom window. At first, she expected him to "put the moves on" and was ready to order him to leave, but Justin would only sleep peacefully beside her bed. She knew Justin was dating a lot of girls, but he only seemed to want to talk to her. Gradually, she went from feeling wary of his advances to being a little annoyed they never came.

Finally, her frustration got the better of her pride and she asked, "Why haven't you ever tried to kiss me?"

Justin smiled. "You and I have become really good friends. I guess I thought if I tried to kiss you–well, you know I get around–I thought you would hate me for taking advantage. I mean, your Mom just died. It didn't seem right."

Although a lot had happened in the ensuing months, nothing had changed between Samantha and

Justin, except that Sam's wisdom and maturity was becoming the driving force behind most of the positive things that Justin did. At one point, Justin had stopped going to high school and no one seemed to notice except Sam. She went to his house and gave him a precocious lecture about the importance of becoming a contributor in the world and not just someone who lived off his mom and dad's fortune.

Justin would not have listened to one-fourth of this sermon from his parents, but he listened to Samantha and returned to school with a completely different attitude. It was at that point that adults started paying attention to Justin again, and he admitted to himself that he liked his teachers' approval. He knew that he had Sam to thank for turning him around. Yet, it would be too much to say Justin's behavior was now perfect.

On the subject of Ms. Doyle, something told Samantha to keep her mouth shut. She quickly considered and dismissed for now the idea of enlisting Justin in the grand project that Ms. Doyle had proposed. It did sound less intimidating with Justin's help. But when she considered how paranoid and reclusive the old woman was, she decided to talk to her first about Justin before divulging Ms. Doyle's secret. After all, it would be understandable if Ms. Doyle were wary of Justin, given his reputation.

She tried to put the subject of Ms. Doyle to rest by saying, "She's a really serious lady, but she seems nice enough."

"Samantha, I really need to talk to you about something that has happened!"

If Samantha were not trying to change the subject, she would have asked him if they could talk later since she was so overwhelmed with all she had taken on in the last couple of days. Instead, she said, "Of course!" and let him inside her house.

After several false starts, Justin finally blurted it out– "Molly is pregnant and I don't know what the hell to do!"

"How could you, Justin?" Samantha sighed. "You told me you were going to be more responsible! What happened to thinking about others' feelings? What happened to considering consequences?" Then, after a pause, and more gently, "What does she want to do?"

"Well, I don't know what she wants to do, but I told her to get an abortion," Justin answered while placing his hands on top of his head.

Sam threw herself on her couch holding her face like she was in pain. In some ways, she was. This was the last thing she needed this week. She then thought about how scared Molly must be.

"How pregnant is she?" Samantha asked. "Where is she now?"

"Well, she thinks she's like two months pregnant, but she doesn't know because she hasn't seen a doctor."

"What?! You need to get her to the doctor immediately and see what's going on. Get her on the phone right now. Get her to come over, so we can figure this out today."

While Justin called Molly, Samantha walked to her bedroom and lay in bed face down. *This is too much responsibility for me!* Sam thought, but in her head she could hear the Jamaican voice of Hyacinth–

"God never give us more than we can handle."

After about three minutes, she walked to the bathroom, turned the faucet on full blast, and threw cold water repeatedly on her face. As she dried her face, Sam returned to the bedroom and sat at her vanity. It had been a week since she had taken time to look at herself. Though she was exhausted, she saw a beautiful young woman looking back at her. She thought she was prettier than just the week before.

She saw her features that resembled her mother. Her long blond hair fell around her round face like her mother's, and she had the same freckles below her eyes and around her nose. Sam remembered her father telling her that she was more and more like her mom.

Samantha was bringing her memory of her mom back to life by displaying the qualities that her mother was known to exhibit on a daily basis, and now she was noticing the physical resemblance more as well. Samantha smiled at herself and felt rejuvenated by her thoughts.

"Time to fix this mess," she said, jumped up and headed towards Justin, who now was in the living room on the phone with his head hung down.

Samantha recognized the importance of her actions and advice in this precarious situation as she sat beside Justin and placed her hand on his shoulder. He looked up at Samantha and, for the first time, she saw tears in his eyes. The neighborhood bad boy was now emotional and frazzled.

"She's about two minutes from here," Justin said. "I don't know what the hell to do."

Samantha looked at him and thought about his statement. "Well, you might not know now, but in the end you will make *the right decision,*" she said as she looked at him sternly.

The doorbell rang as soon as Samantha finished her sentence. As she walked to the door she realized she hadn't thought for herself what she was going to say to Molly. Right then and there she considered her own beliefs about abortion–not realizing that they were really Hyacinth's views–and what she would do if she was the one in that situation.

I'm still a damn virgin! Sam thought. *How am I supposed to put myself in her shoes?*

The door swung open to reveal a five-foot-tall young woman who could easily be mistaken for a child. Molly was not like the rest of privileged children in Greenwich. She was the daughter of a Mexican house maid for one of the richest men in the U.S. Although she, her mother, and her brother had lived on the Pagoda Estate from the time she was an infant, the Pagodas always treated all of them, not just her mother, like the help. Every time they acted like this was their own neighborhood, they were reminded of their low place in this upper-class world. Two years before, when Molly started dating a different boy from the neighborhood, not only did his family threaten to disown him, but Mr. Pagoda told Molly's mother that she would lose her job if she didn't put a stop to the "inappropriate relationship."

After that day, Molly stuck to "her own kind" and went to the predominately Latino neighborhood a town over for school dances and other social functions. Molly took her unfair treatment to heart and hated everyone from Greenwich until she met Justin walking home. Justin made her laugh by making fun of Greenwich and the jaded lives of its inhabitants, including those of his own parents, who were both rumored to be having affairs. She quickly fell in love with the handsome and loquacious boy who seemed to feel the same way about their neighborhood, even though he was not treated like an outsider. But Justin never loved her the way she loved him.

When she saw Justin sitting on the couch, she hurried toward him with tears streaming down her face.

"I know you hate me for this," Molly said as she sat beside Justin. "I don't want to ruin your life or mine. But I really don't know what to do."

"I don't know what to do either. I don't hate you Molly," Justin said in the most sincere voice Samantha had ever heard from him. "I just have no idea how to fix this."

They both started to cry. Justin pulled Molly closer to him and held her tightly.

Samantha sat across from them but could feel the anguish they were experiencing. Samantha did what she did whenever she needed to think clearly in complicated, real-time situations. She channeled the spirit of Hyacinth to help her.

"The first thing you guys need to do is realize that this is a child we are talking about," Sam said. "This is a decision that needs to be well thought out. You need to find a doctor and have them examine you to make sure you and the baby are okay. I understand that you are afraid of what the future holds, but you have to do what's right, no matter what your families think.

The thought about her mother made Molly cringe at the last part of Samantha's statement.

"I want to have an abortion before my mother finds out that I'm pregnant," Molly said as she wiped her tears. "She would just die if she ever found out."

"In the end it's not going to be your families who would be committing a sin if you decide to have an abortion," Samantha added. "Not your mother, not your father. Only you. Your act. Your sin."

"So what do you suggest we do, Sam?"

They all sat in silence for a full two minutes. It was obvious Sam was deep in thought. Justin finally grew impatient and turned to Molly and asked her what she wanted to do. Samantha had no solution, but one thing she knew was that there were other options besides abortion.

"I really don't want an abortion," Molly said. "But I just can't see another way out."

"There's other ways to do this," Samantha quickly answered. "We just have to figure it out together. Did you graduate high school this year or are you in the same class as Justin?"

I'm going into the twelfth grade," Molly answered. "What other ways are you talking about?"

Samantha tried to figure out how Molly could have the baby without disrupting her schooling.

"Well, let's just get you to a doctor, and we will start from there," Samantha said. "We need to find out if everything is OK before we jump to any conclusions. I'll call a clinic in Portchester and set an appointment for early next week. We can go together. Until then, you two need to support each other and talk. Hyacinth would always say, 'Sometimes good blessings come in bad disguises.'"

Samantha's words calmed Molly's troubled mind. Molly always thought that a child would be a blessing, but only when she was married and settled into her career as doctor. Justin never looked at children as a blessing. He always thought they were a burden that people trapped themselves into.

"Come on, let me take you home," Justin said.

"I drove here, Justin," Molly said. Are you okay?"

"No I am not, but I am trying to be," he said. "This is just messing with my mind. Let me ride home with you, and I'll walk back home."

After Molly walked over to Sam, crouched over and hugged her, Justin and Molly made their way to the door as Samantha sat there still thinking about what would happen. She knew Justin still did not want Molly to have the child after seeing how he reacted to her words. If anyone needed convincing, it would be Justin. It's not like Samantha thought abortion was *always* wrong. If there was something definitely wrong with the child, she would support it.

5

AMALGAMATE

It was time for Samantha to head to the Bronx for my second lesson. Sam was thinking about her father's happy mood at home. Although she hated him shadowing her, she decided to call her father to see if he would accompany her again. As much as she wanted to travel on her own for once, Sam realized that there was something in it for her father too.

For the first time since her mother died, she noticed her father was excited about life. She knew very well that it had something to do with my Mamma. As soon as she asked him to accompany her, her father quickly accepted and immediately left the department store where he was shopping to rush home and pick up Sam. It was his first time buying clothes for himself in over five years, and it was not going well anyway. Sam made her way up the stairs thinking about what she could bring to enhance my lesson, but before she could change clothes, she heard her father honking the horn of the car like he was late for his own wedding.

It was evident that Mr. Raider liked Gina, but when Samantha mentioned his change of mood, he pretended that his positive outlook was no big deal. Once in the car, Sam thought about sharing her tumultuous morning with her father, but thought there was a chance it might change his mood for the worse. Although she was close with her father, Sam recognized that he would consider Ms. Doyle's international philanthropy idea and Justin and Molly's pregnancy as burdens far too great for his baby girl. She also feared he would accuse her of meddling in other people's problems.

As she sat by her father in the car deciding what she could and couldn't tell him, Mr. Raider realized for himself that something was up with Sam. Usually, she would be the first one to instigate catching up on the day's events when they saw each other later in the day so he knew. They were close like that, because most of the time, they seemed to only have each other now that Hyacinth was gone.

"Is everything okay Sam?" Mr. Raider asked after ten minutes of driving and not a word from Sam. "You're never this quiet."

"Just have a lot on my mind." Sam answered. "I'm not sure what I got myself into when I decided to do this project of mine."

"Well, just remember it's a side project. Don't let it interfere with your schooling," Mr. Raider said. "After school starts, you won't have time for a lot of the things you're doing right now."

Sam thought about what her dad was saying but she knew her father always sympathized with Ms. Doyle and thought what happened to her was very unfortunate.

"Ms. Doyle wants me to give away most of the stuff she has collected over the years," Sam blurted as the car got on the I-95 freeway that led towards the Bronx. "And she has *a lot of stuff.*"

"What to do you mean *a lot of stuff?*" Mr. Raider mocked.

"She is a hoarder," Sam said. "I think she might have things from the eighties in that house!"

Mr. Raider laughed at the word "hoarder," but inside he felt bad about Ms. Doyle's misfortunes. He himself had suffered years of depression after Sam's mother died.

"Losing the person you love is hard to bear," Mr. Raider said as he shook his head. "It can drive you crazy. Only the strongest can survive losing a soul-mate. If you weren't in my life, I'm not sure what I would have done when your mother was killed."

Samantha had been worried about bringing up the subject of Ms. Doyle, but she hadn't foreseen this outcome. Her dad, who was so upbeat about seeing my Mamma again, was now once again dejected about the loss of his wife. Samantha tried to change the subject quickly before they arrived at my house.

"I wonder what Gina has cooked today?" she said in an excited voice. "That food was unbelievable the last time, wasn't it?"

Mr. Raider seemed to be in some kind of trance and kept his head straight, looking at the road without answering Sam.

"Dad! Didn't you hear me?"

"*Ya,* I heard you," he answered in a somber voice. "I'm thinking about your mother. I miss her so badly."

"What did you buy for Gina?" Samantha asked, still trying to change the subject.

"I bought her a massaging cushion from Brookstones. She said her back hurts a lot from work, so I hoped this might help."

"Aww, you're so thoughtful dad," Samantha said. "You really like her don't you?"

It worked. Mr. Raider smiled and looked out the window at a fog covered New York City. He wondered if there was a future for him. *Samantha is so dear,* he thought, grateful that his daughter did not resent his interest in a woman other than her mother. Sam was glad he thinking forward again, rather than backwards. Only ten minutes from my house now, Samantha began to consider how significant it was for her father to be interested in someone and how it might affect their lives.

The details of Sam's mother's death, her father's lack of interest in any other woman up to this point, were still inexplicable to Samantha and to others who knew him well. Samantha never questioned her father about his disinterest in remarrying, but suggested many times that it wouldn't be wrong to give someone else a chance. For the first time, Sam considered her father might have thought that he failed in protecting her mother and feared the possibility that it could happen again.

When they arrived on the city block where my building stood, Mr. Raider looked around carefully for any suspected danger before exiting the car. This was nothing new to Samantha, but it was part of the reason why she had chosen to go to Julliard and travel to New York City by herself. The overprotective behavior was beyond annoying to Sam, who just wanted to live a normal life now that she wasn't a child anymore. *Could a relationship with Gina help Dad accept that I am growing up and can take care of myself?* Sam mused. Waiting for a group of boys to walk past them, Sam impetuously jumped out the car and started to walk towards the building. Mr. Raider came running out of the car behind her, frustrated that she had once again defied his command to stay close.

"Not everyone in the world is bad, Dad," Sam yelled as he came up and put his hand on her shoulder.

Knowing there was no way he would win that argument, Mr. Raider kept his mouth shut and walked behind Sam to our front door. Ecstatic to see Sam again, I quickly grabbed her hand and brought her to the dinner table. I had several pages of sheet music that my mother had bought for me at the music store the day before. I spent night and day studying practicing and learned all my notes well. When she looked at the table and picked up one of the sheets of music, she realized how serious I was about mastering the violin. At that point, it was the only thing I wanted to do.

"I'm happy that the violin has such an impact on you already," Sam said, while looking at one of the sheets of paper.

"Playing the violin makes me feel so good," I responded. "I love the way it sounds close to my ear. I want to play all the time. I want to be the best violinist ever!"

"Well, let's get to it then!" Sam said as she sat down at the table, smiling.

I could hear Mr. Raider talking to my mother in the background. I looked over to Mamma and saw that she was just as happy as I was. It was a good day in our home. It seemed that we were finally getting what we wanted.

Sam and I were distracted by Mamma shredding the tightly wrapped gift paper. When she opened the package and saw what was in it, she looked up at Mr. Raider in shock.

"I thought that you needed something like this for the aches and pain you get from working," Mr. Raider said.

"This was very thoughtful of you, Martin," Mamma said, then moved to hug him.

At first he moved away, but then he caught himself and leaned toward Mamma to accept the embrace. It was the first time I had seen my mother hug a man in three years.

They held each other for a surprisingly long time before Mamma broke off the embrace and said, "Let me cook for you."

"Well, I was thinking that after Sam and Ophelia finish up, we could go out to dinner," Mr. Raider said as he walked towards us. "Hello, Ophelia. Do you want to go out to dinner, little lady?"

I nodded my head, my mother got tense. I knew what she was thinking.

"We have nothing to wear," Mamma said. "Can we go another day?"

"Well, none of us have dress clothes," Mr. Raider answered. "Why don't we stop at the stores in SoHo so we can all buy something to wear? Then, we can have some *real* Chinese food in Chinatown."

My mother looked over towards me. I nodded my head vigorously, praying she wouldn't pass up on what was becoming one of the best days we would have that year. Seeing how bad I wanted it, she turned to Mr. Raider.

"I will go only if you let me do something to repay you," she said to him. "Let me come and clean your house or something."

"Deal," Mr. Raider said.

Mamma and Mr. Raider vigorously talked while I screeched away at the violin and soaked up everything Sam taught me. After an hour, we all headed out to downtown Manhattan. Sam and I sat in the back of car, as Mamma sat up front with Mr. Raider. Mamma laughed at Mr. Raider's jokes about how hard it was to be a single dad with a strong headed daughter. Sam defended herself by telling Mamma how overprotective he was, which made her laugh even harder. When Sam described how Mr. Raider peeked out their front door before he exited his own home and would almost run to his car, locking the door behind him in the driveway–all of this in Greenwich, mind you–Mamma became hysterical with laughter. Pretty soon, we were all laughing as we traveled on FDR Drive down to SoHo.

It was seven in the evening, but in the middle of summer it might as well have been 10:00 AM. Every store was open and they were all packed with shoppers. After pulling into a parking spot and Mr. Raider paying more money for parking than my mother had spent for food for that entire week, we made our way into the store, but abruptly, Sam grabbed my hand and quickly took me across the street into a store more appropriate for girls our age.

Before even looking for anything for herself, she started to pick out several dresses for me to try. I couldn't help but imagine every day being like this one from that day on. After we chose a dress for me, one in a pastel pink that puffed out and was fun to spin in, Sam walked to the back of the store to find matching shoes, stockings and hat. She then quickly picked out a little black dress for herself. We walked to the front of the store where she handed the storekeeper her credit card.

"We will be wearing these out of here," Sam said to the woman, who gave us bags to put the clothes we were wearing before.

"Thank you so much Sam," I said. Words could not describe how grateful I was for everything she was doing, but I tried anyway. "You have been like an angel to me."

"It's nothing, Ophelia," she answered. "I'll pick out more clothes you can wear back to school while you put on your new dress."

Two bags of stylish new school clothes and an outfit fit for a princess, were enough to make me feel like walking on air. I couldn't wait for my mother to see me. We found her in a dressing room, with a saleswoman zipping the back of her dress. I spun in a circle around after I caught her attention.

"I haven't seen you dressed up in such a long time," she said as her eyes swelled with tears.

"You look beautiful too, Mamma," I said, as I looked at the form-fitting dress with thin leather strips running through it. We all met up, looking flawless and started to walk towards the restaurants of Chinatown. Mr. Raider was wearing a bright floral tie with a black sports jacket and slacks.

I remember everything from that evening, especially the hanging roasted pigs in every restaurant window we passed. It seemed like we were overdressed for the area we were in. The smelled of fish and rotten food permeated the air. Markets carried everything from Chinese baked goods to fruits and vegetables I had never seen before. We soon walked onto a street that seemed fit for our attire. We entered a restaurant with huge tanks of live seafood lining the front waiting area. People of all cultures sat there eating, but as soon as we walked in, we became the center of attention. A Chinese girl dressed in full cultural attire greeted us and led us to our table. Mr.

Raider was a gentleman every step of the way, pulling out Mamma's chair, then helping Samantha and I into ours. A menu written in Chinese and English was placed in front of us, but we gave them back to the waiter after Mr. Raider asked permission to order for us. When the food came out, Mamma marveled at the look of it.

"So this is what *real* Chinese food looks like," she blurted. "This is not what they sell in the corner stores in the Bronx."

"Is it not the same?" Mr. Raider asked.

"Nope. In the Bronx, it's filled with MSG and bad oil that they fry everything in," she explained. "This smells and looks completely different."

Five different kinds of entrees including duck and lobster were served with sides of rice, noodles, and vegetables. Mamma enjoyed every bite she took. We all did.

"Let's make this our tradition," Mr. Raider said.

I felt good that he was looking towards the future and we were in it. Mamma agreed with Mr. Raider.

While they shared a bottle of wine, it was almost like they were the only ones there. Mr. Raider took care of the bill while Mamma made sure the waitress put every grain of rice into containers, explaining that the food was too good to let any of it go to waste.

"You want to order some more to go, Gina?" Mr. Raider asked, smiling at her vigilance over making sure everything was saved.

"There's so much here already," she said then paused considering the question. "Maybe some more of that shrimp fried rice to compliment all this meat we're taking."

We brought the food back to the car. Sam tried to keep the night going by suggesting we go see a play or a movie on Broadway. Mamma had work the next day, but made it clear that she had not had a night out in three years, so if it meant going to work the next day tired, then so be it. A quick drive north on Broadway through a blur of city lights landed us on 43rd Street, where Mr. Raider bought Les Misérables tickets at prices that made Mamma wide eyed.

A perfect day topped off with a beautiful and

stunning musical. "It doesn't get any better than this!" I exclaimed. Everyone smiled in agreement.

That night, as I watched the actors performing on stage and receiving a standing ovation at the end, I imagined myself performing in front of thousands of people. Within one week, I had discovered what I wanted to do for my career. I thanked God for leading us to that violin and Sam and Mr. Raider.

6
The Savior

It seemed strange returning to our neighborhood and apartment after spending the night out. Mamma said she felt like Cinderella returning from the ball. Yes, we were returning to our reality, and our reality involved hearing gunshots and police sirens–sometimes all night, but once again we had caught a glimpse of the other side. After years of enduring it, gunshots were like shutters clattering in the wind, sirens like one of those white-noise machines people use to put themselves to sleep.

For Mamma, it was a different story. She had lost a brother to the streets of The Bronx when she was sixteen. She had told me about the night he came running into the house covered in blood. She had heard the gunshots outside the house and barely flinched, but seeing her brother bleed to death had traumatized her irreparably. The sound of bullets could send her into a catatonic trance for minutes.

Usually, I would have to go to Mamma and stroke her hair, telling her everything was okay until she came around. But that night, she didn't freeze up. She got angry when the guns fired and the boys ran through the building. I knew exactly why she was different this time. It was obvious that the evening had given her a new lease on life and was now looking forward to better times with or without Mr. Raider.

"Andeldiablo! We need to move out of here ASAP, Ophelia, before these animals kill us along with themselves," Mamma fumed.

Huddled in the back room to avoid getting shot through the front window, I had grabbed my violin before taking my customary gunshot spot beside her on the floor in the bedroom we shared. Mamma didn't stay angry long though. Instead, she opened the box with the massager, spread it out on her bed, and laid on it.

"This feels like heaven," she murmured over the hum of the machine. "It's amazing the way this day turned out, isn't it?"

"Ya," I answered distractedly. I had been trying to remember everything Sam taught me earlier that evening while I stroked the violin with a bow.

"Keep playing," Mamma said. "Music to my ears. It's amazing how quick you are learning. I am so proud of you."

I was already starting to get the screeching under control. I adjusted my grip and concentrated on moving the bow parallel to the strings to make the sound sweet and avoid that horrible noise.

Mamma fell asleep after ten minutes of massage, but I stayed up for two more hours playing the violin until my fingers could take no more. That night, I thanked God for Sam and her father as I looked at my mother laying there. It was the earliest she had fallen asleep in weeks. Her aches and pain bothered her so much that sometimes she wouldn't fall asleep without the help of two or three painkillers.

The next morning, Sam accompanied Molly to the doctor as promised. Sam was the one that stood firmly by her while the female doctor examined Molly for the first time. According to the doctor, all was well with her and the baby. Sam and Molly exited the doctor's office expecting to see Justin waiting in the lobby seat where they left him. After a few minutes looking around the halls, calling into the restroom, and circling the building, they accepted that Justin was nowhere to be found and resolved to leave in Sam's car. Before Molly had her seatbelt on, her face was wet.

"He's going to run," Molly exclaimed through her tears. "He's not going to stay with us." Sam gathered from this "us" that Molly was now thinking of the fetus as a child and wanted the support of Justin.

"It doesn't matter if he's there for you," Sam said. "This is your child. We'll figure it out together."

Molly was comforted by Sam's confidence and started to express relief that her and the baby were okay.

"I agree with you Sam," Molly said. "It's not about what my family thinks. This is my decision…that will affect me for the rest of my life. I don't think I could live with myself knowing that I did something as gruesome as abort a baby more than two months along."

"I've been thinking of a few options and was waiting until today to talk to you about them," Sam said. "I was thinking you could drop out of high school and take the GED immediately, so you can attend college in upper Connecticut. You can kind of hide away from everyone until you give birth. I'm sure by then your mom would be okay with the baby if she sees you making it on your own. Because your mother doesn't have a large income, you can take student loans from the government to pay your bills. I would help you with the baby and do anything else I could."

"*Wow*, I can see why Justin chose you for this," Molly said, turning towards Sam and looking directly into her eyes. "You really have it all together don't you?"

"Well, not *all* together, but I had no choice but to learn to think for myself," Sam answered as she smiled at the compliment. "After my mother died, I had to become a mother to myself and to my father. I had no choice but to grow up fast and take control of my life."

"I'm sorry about your mom," Molly answered in a somber tone. "Justin told me all about it. Did they ever find the killer?"

"Not that I know of," Sam said. "It makes me angry that whoever it is still walks free. But Hyacinth told me to give it up to God. 'Let *Him* fight your battles,' she used to say."

After Samantha finished telling Molly about Hyacinth, she told her that if didn't want to keep the baby, there were many families who couldn't have children who would readily adopt the baby after it was born. Molly entertained the idea for about a minute, but then said "I would worry that the person wouldn't take care of the child the way they should." By the time they arrived home, Molly had determined that she was going to raise the baby. She was still concerned about her mother, though, who didn't handle stress well. Samantha opined to Molly that it was important that she did what's best for everyone involved and to hide it from her mother if she wouldn't be helpful.

Samantha didn't discuss what Justin had done, knowing it would only upset Molly, but after Molly exited the car, Sam raced home, parked, and stomped her way to Justin's front door. She rang the bell twice, peeking through the stained glass window in it to see if he was hiding inside. After she saw Justin ducking behind the living room couch, Sam started to scream.

"Come out here now, or the entirety of Greenwich is going to know what you did!" Within seconds, the door was flung open. Justin came flying out, grabbing Sam by the hand, pulling her away from the front door.

"My Dad is upstairs," he whispered. "Have you lost your mind?"

"No, you've lost your mind!" she answered. "How dare you leave Molly at the doctor's office like a coward?! What does that say about you as a person?"

"I was so scared that I couldn't think of anything but to run. I ran all the way home," Justin said. "This is too much for me!"

"Well you need to prepare yourself, because the fetus is healthy, and it sounds like Molly is going to push through and have the baby one way or the other."

Justin fell to his knees right there on the sidewalk.

"I'm ruined," he said as he looked up at Sam, "My Dad's going to disown me."

"Pull yourself together, and get up off the ground," Sam said. "Stop thinking about yourself for a change. What are you afraid of? Losing your weekly allowance, so you can't buy any more video games? There are more important things to life than what you have been doing. Look at this as God trying to tell you it's time to let go of your childish ways."

Justin said nothing. He stood up to his feet, took a long look at Sam, and then walked away. The look he gave Sam was enough for her to sit there and watch him go. It was menacing. Sam knew right then and there Justin was not in a right frame of mind. That desperate, threatening glare was not what she expected from him.

She watched him walk slowly back to his door. She almost called his name but thought better of it. He closed the door behind him. Sam made her way home.

As soon as she reached the front door, she was greeted by a letter wedged in the doorjamb. The letter was from Ms. Doyle, demanding that she stop by some time before day's end. *Not right now,* she thought.

Sam was confident Molly was going to be okay, but felt sure she was going to lose Justin, whom she was just starting to think of as her best friend. Saddened by his behavior and hurt by that look he gave her, she threw herself in her bed, face first, but she did not cry. Instead, she reached over for her iPad and put on some soothing music. Suddenly, she wondered just how Ms. Doyle was getting these notes to her house. She knew the woman never left the house. Intrigued by her demand, Sam jumped up and made her way to the Doyle mansion.

Once again, as soon as she arrived at the gate, it swung open. The reclusive woman came walking towards her in a black nightgown. It was obvious Ms. Doyle had done nothing to her hair since their last visit. She was in the same disheveled state.

"Why haven't you come to help me?" Ms. Doyle asked. Sam was becoming an expert at changing the subject. "Can you bring me to that beautiful garden of yours, Ms. Doyle?" she asked.

Caught by surprise, Ms. Doyle turned quickly and walked toward the garden. Sam hoped the beautiful scenery would calm her down. As soon as she entered the greenhouse, Ms. Doyle picked up a large pair of scissors and started to prune her way around the perimeter.

"Who helps you with the garden, Ms. Doyle?" Sam asked.

"Well, I have a group of workmen coming in twice a week," she answered. "I communicate what needs to be done over the phone. You want to know how those notes are making their way to your door, don't you."

"Kinda," Sam answered. "Actually, I'm stumped."

"Well, you'll only get notes Tuesdays and Thursdays, because those are their work days," Ms. Doyle answered. "They also deliver my groceries if you must know."

"Tell me about these plants over here," Sam said, looking at a weird-shaped, cactus-like plant she had never seen before.

Ms. Doyle's eyes lit up as she told Sam about the *Aloe vera* plant and its medicinal uses as she snipped a piece. Sam at least for the moment, felt she had Ms. Doyle in the palm of her hands. It wasn't just a ploy, though. Sam really was interested in the vast greenhouse full of life. They spent the next hour talking about horticulture until Ms. Doyle grew tired and took a seat in the back of the greenhouse that overlooked several rows of small trees outside.

"Have you given thought to my request?" Ms. Doyle asked as she put her feet up on a stool.

"Not much, but I have," Sam said standing beside her. "I think to fix your immediate clutter issue, you should have a yard sale."

"That's the best you could come up with? Really!" Ms. Doyle scoffed. "As I told you before, I want my things to go to people who really need them, not some ass who's trying to make a quick buck."

"Not everyone is like that, Ms. Doyle," Sam said. "I have met several people at our yard sales who could not afford nice things otherwise, even some who came to our yard sale looking for something worthwhile to give to others. How do you think I got my idea in the first place?"

"Well, I haven't met many people in this country who haven't had some ulterior motive," Ms. Doyle insisted.

"But some ulterior motives can be altruistic too!" Sam proclaimed. "Take this family I've grown very fond of. Gina found my violin at our yard sale, and now it's her daughter's prized possession. Her daughter, Ophelia, has been studying very hard and shows real promise. In the process of teaching Ophelia, my Dad and Gina have become close friends. My father has been without companionship as long as you have! As it turns out, giving that violin to them has blessed us at least as much as…"

"I don't want to know how your yard sale went," Ms. Doyle interrupted. "I have bigger and better ideas than you, my little dear. I don't just want to get rid of my *clutter*, as you so delicately put it. This is my philanthropic vision!"

Sam darted a quick angry look at her and stormed off.

Ms. Doyle caught herself. "Sam, please. I didn't mean that. Come back and talk to me. Please." And then, as if to herself, she added, "I don't know why I do that."

"Probably because you're a mean and bitter woman," Sam replied as she turned around.

Ms. Doyle paused. "That's a fair assessment. But please be patient with me. I am contemplating a lot of change! I wasn't always like this, you know. You remind me so much of myself when I was younger."

Sam stood there pondering for a moment, then walked back to Ms. Doyle, who beckoned her to come inside for a cup of peppermint tea from mint she had just picked from the garden. Sam could not resist Ms. Doyle's likening of her younger self, a brilliant designer and business woman. Also, she couldn't resist the freshly brewed tea, which offered some comfort in what had become a very stressful day. The tea reminded her of Hyacinth, who used to pick mint from her backyard and bring it to the Raider home every Saturday morning.

As they walked toward the kitchen, Sam apologized to Ms. Doyle for her insult. She was remembering what her father said–that her situation was not completely of her own making. Sam realized what Ms. Doyle said must be true–she must have been a different person when she was younger. An antisocial person could not have had such success in the considerably publicized fashion world. Sam also surmised that somewhere inside Ms. Doyle, there must have been a lot of good left in her to want to share her belonging and wealth with the entire world, even if she was emphasizing that the beneficiaries needed to be trustworthy.

"Ms. Doyle, I know you're a good woman," Sam said. "Someone told me a long time ago that we can't let the devil get the best of us. You can't let what happened years ago prevent you from living and being happy in this life."

"Why was Justin kneeling down in front of you earlier?" Doyle asked. "How about you? Was that *you* letting what happened years ago prevent you from being happy? Or were you just giving an asshole what was coming to him?"

"Hardly…that's not my…but…wait a minute! You were spying on us from your window!"

"Guilty as charged," grinned Ms. Doyle, as they shared a hearty laugh.

Over tea, Sam told the story of her friendship with Justin, but stopped short of telling her about the pregnancy.

"That Justin is no good," Ms. Doyle said. "How

can you blame him, though? Just look at his mother and father. His mother is as selfish and pleasure-seeking as they come. And the father, well, he is certifiable. I saw him kill the boy's dog with a shovel, screaming about the dog shitting on the porch. He buried it right back there where his son could find the grave!

Sam was dumbfounded. "Why didn't you do something?" she asked.

Ms. Doyle continued. "I picked up the phone, but before I could figure out who to call. Would the police insist on interviewing me? Would Justin's dad come after me? I just shut down and did nothing. I'm so embarrassed."

"Does Justin know it was his dad?" Samantha asked.

"I don't know Samantha. But I'll tell you this–I feel bad for Justin, but he scares me too. I don't think the apple fell too far from the tree."

Confusion turned to fear. She knew that Justin was capable of being cruel but she never thought of him as violent. Ms. Doyle's words made her worry about Molly.

The look on her face soon drew the attention of Ms. Doyle. "You okay, Sam?"

Maybe I shouldn't keep all of this to myself, Sam thought. She was keeping information about Ms. Doyle from her father and Justin, as well as information about Justin and Molly from Ms. Doyle. It is one thing to respect people's privacy, but she was starting to feel overwhelmed.

"Sam?"

Sam blurted it out. "Justin got Molly pregnant."

"Oh Lord!" Doyle exclaimed.

"They are scared to tell their parents, but I at least talked them into going to the doctor."

"What did the doctor say?"

"Everything seems to be OK, but Justin ran off before the doctor said that. Molly felt abandoned, and I just thought he was being so self-centered, so I was telling him how I felt about his disgusting behavior. He usually listens to me, but this time I guess I pushed too hard when I threatened to tell his parents. He gave me the scariest look I've ever seen and walked away."

"Normally, I would be calling the boy's parents right now, no matter what you wanted me to do," Ms. Doyle said. "But not these parents." She paused. "It's half their fault. This was bound to happen with all of those girls coming in and out of his house like that with no grownups around. That poor sweet thing."

Samantha started to tear up. "Maybe I should have just stayed out of it."

Ms. Doyle put down her napkin and moved closer to Samantha to comfort her. The hard shell that Ms. Doyle had encased herself in was starting to crack. Of course, part of it was sympathy with Molly regarding how alone she must feel being in trouble with such a selfish boy, and only being able to confide in Samantha, who she barely knew. She also felt some remorse about the anger she had expressed towards Samantha for not coming to see her sooner when Sam was dealing with so much drama but there was also something else. How cruel it felt to Ms. Doyle that

God had not granted her a child but had given one to these kids who were not ready. Ms. Doyle's drift towards self-pity was interrupted when Sam's whole body jerked. Sam had an idea!

"Ms. Doyle, do you think you might allow me to have an assistant to help with your project?"

"It depends who it is," Ms. Doyle answered. Keep in mind you will be responsible for their actions if you vouch for them. I know that boy Justin is strong, but I just don't feel…

"No, not Justin!" Sam stated. "Molly! I know I don't know her that well, but I think she really needs this. I can't believe she'd do anything to mess it up."

"Doesn't her mother works for the Pagodas?" Ms. Doyle asked. "They are the worst."

"That's her," Sam answered. "If they find out what happened, her mother will be fired. Molly says she can't even tell her mom."

"Well, let's think about it," Ms. Doyle paused. "I want to meet her."

"Okay. I'll only ask her to help with your big yard sale for now."

"When did I agree to a yard sale?!" Ms. Doyle asked.

Faced with the near-magical force of Samantha's personality, Ms. Doyle did end up agreeing to the yard sale. Even in a neighborhood already famous for yard sales, it would be the biggest one ever. Before Sam left Ms. Doyle that day, they had picked a date just two Saturdays away. They also called an event company to rent two large tents and hired all the manpower from two different moving companies. They would come on Friday and early Saturday for muscle to get everything in place. They also had a plan for how most of the items would be arranged. Ms. Doyle was left with the task of determining prices.

When Sam got home, her father was nowhere to be found. Usually she would arrive home to at least dinner and a movie, but that night, Mr. Raider had promised Mamma he would pick her up from work in Greenwich and take her back to the Bronx to save her the one-hour bus ride. Sam had forgotten, but she was only lonely for a few seconds before she was overtaken by gratitude. This was the first time her father had been out with someone other than herself in seven years. And the timing could not have been better. If her meeting with Ms. Doyle had not ended so satisfactorily, she would have needed him. As it was, she was glad she didn't have to decide what to tell him. Their ritual "How was your day" debriefing might have gone South. Instead, she raided the fridge and went right to bed.

Sam awakened in the middle of the night thinking about Justin. She texted him, but he didn't answer. Lying there in bed, she thought about what might have happened if he had kissed her when she wanted him to. She felt conflicted. She was still angry with him–maybe even a little scared of him–but she tried to dismiss that thought. Mostly, she was grateful that he had gone against his habits, and maybe even his very nature, by putting her needs above his own at that time. She began to worry about him and texted him again with no luck.

Why didn't I have any more serious crushes? Why didn't I have any close friends–unless Justin counted. I didn't even go to prom, she thought, *and I love to dance!*

That was it. She was so focused on herself and her activities, first on dancing and violin, then just dancing, that she didn't really miss having a "*BFF*" or a boyfriend. Hyacinth had warned her that she needed to give time to others or she would one day lose herself, but until now, that advice had gone in one ear and out the other.

Sam thought about all the things she had missed out on by practicing violin and especially dance almost every available moment. She had never been so happy to be a virgin as today, but she hadn't even experienced her first kiss. What would it be like to be with someone she really loved, really wanted *in that way*. Maybe, she would meet someone at Juilliard who could understand her focus and drive. Maybe, she would meet a handsome dancer, fall in love, and live happily ever after. She drifted back asleep into dreams that, while not exactly peaceful, were very sweet.

7

THE HIDDEN

Soon, Mr. Raider was bringing my mother home from work every night, greeting her with a wrapped present, which he told her to open after he was gone. As tired as Mamma was from work, her mind raced at the thought of what could be in the box. She opened it as soon as she walked through the door and discovered it contained a pair of shoes that were more comfortable than anything she had ever worn.

He had gone back to the same sales lady who had helped Mamma that first night out in Chinatown to get Mamma's size. For a while, all the gifts revolved around making sure Mamma was comfortable–a nice pair of sunglasses, new pillows for the bed, and a fancy showerhead to take advantage of that awesome New York City water pressure. But then, he raised the stakes.

We had returned to the same fancy Chinatown restaurant as before, and after we had been seated, he pulled a box out of his right pocket and sat it on the table in front of Mamma. The pastel blue box was too big for an engagement ring, and not exactly being a frequent Tiffany's customer, Mamma did not know what to expect, but Samantha's eyes got wide as saucers. As she began to open the box, Mr. Raider plopped down identical blue boxes in front of Sam and me. I couldn't help but kick back my chair and stand up–I was so excited. In the three boxes, we found matching diamond Tiffany bracelets with our names engraved on them. At that point, I thought this man was a God amongst men.

Mamma shocked me by standing up and circling the table so that she could plant a long, soft kiss on his lips. Once again, we were the main attraction in the restaurant because of my jumping up and down and squealing. Sam grabbed my arm and gave me a firm yet sweet look that said, "use your inside voice." Mamma was tearing up, not so much because of the expense but because of the meaningful gesture, which gave physical proof to the bond that was forming between us all.

The only time I remember Mamma showing any strong affection in public was the day I had my tonsils removed and was coming back from the hospital on the bus. She had kissed me on my forehead as a way of saying sorry that she had been so grumpy about the long bus trips we had to take since we couldn't afford a cab.

I was sure my normally reserved mother was in love with Mr. Raider when she kissed him like that! The way they stared at each other through dinner played right into my fairytale fantasy. Sam and I knew there was something special going on. *Were we going to be sisters?*! Earlier, between corrections and pointers on the violin, she expressed amazement about how much time Mr. Raider was spending away from home, and told me how mopey he was before he had met my mother. The person I knew was nothing like the "zombie" Samantha described. We never made it home that night. Sam begged Mamma and me to spend the night at their house to help her with Ms. Doyle's yard sale that next morning. After some begging from me and blushing encouragement from Mr. Raider, Mamma agreed. After a trip uptown for fancy frozen yogurt, we made our way to where the other half lived.

We arrived at the house around 10 p.m., tired from all the excitement. But once the door was open to the huge house, Mamma and I wanted to explore this dream home from the movies. The "grand tour" revealed two things Mr. Raider obsessed over. The first was his collection of fine art. The second was everything being in exactly the right place. In response to Mr. Raider's admission that he might be "a bit particular about how things are arranged,"

Samantha began imitating a pretentious host. In her best Academy Award voice, she awarded him the prize for "greatest understatement of all time!" We all laughed hysterically—even Mr. Raider.

Mr. Raider had paintings and sculptures from a bunch of famous artists that I had never heard of. I couldn't believe it when Samantha said the beautiful, naked lady in several of the portraits was of her mother. Mamma and I looked at each other, exchanging scandalous looks of surprise and amazement, but I could tell Mamma liked it.

I had so much fun! Mr. Raider laughed at our mock disapproval and explained that, as a well-known ballerina, his wife had been a muse for several artists in New York City. We watched him examine each painting from several angles, correcting any crookedness. He picked up tiny pieces of lint or paper and put them in his pocket. Mamma and I both noted this fussiness with raised eyebrows. When I mentioned it to Mamma later, she said it was a good thing that he was a clean man.

"Remember Sweetie, I work for people who strip themselves wherever they happen to be and leave everything on the floor until I show up to pick it up," Mamma said. "I'll take a neat freak over a pig any day."

If Mamma was happy with it, then fine, but it was strange to me because my father was the opposite of Mr. Raider in every way I could think of.

That night, we were given more evidence of Mr. Raider's intense nature. He had arranged relics from an earlier period in his life into a glass case–golf trophies, pictures of him with famous people like Mayor Koch, and a certificate recognizing his service as the CEO of a banking firm. Strangely, these mementos said "La Roche" rather than "Raider." Sam explained that Mr. Raider had changed their names to signify starting over when they lost her mother, and chose her maiden name as a tribute. Mamma was touched by the depth of the gesture.

"So I finally found out what you did before you retired," Mamma said as she looked at the certificate.

Mr. Raider nodded without a smile and quickly changed the subject to his collection of rare, first-edition books. Then, he and Samantha brought us upstairs to see the seven bedrooms on the second floor. I wondered why such a small family would want seven bedrooms to maintain. Sam told me how her dad became detached from his life when her mother died–no golf, no work, no social functions, nor visits from family or friends. What good was all this room if you never had visitors?

After the tour of the house, Mr. Raider showed us to separate bedrooms, while Sam brought us nightwear from Mr. Raider's closet for Mamma and from her own for me. She still seemed happy, but Mr. Raider's mood had soured as we left the study. I asked Sam about it, because it made me feel uncomfortable. He had just wandered off, leaving it to Sam to show us to our rooms. He hadn't even wished us goodnight.

"My father doesn't do well with the past," she said. "He *really* doesn't like talking about banking."

Sam said he use to really like banking, but she had learned to avoid the subject. She didn't know why he didn't want to talk about it. In fact, Mr. Raider's past seemed to be cloudy in a lot of ways.

"Just try to talk to Dad about the here and now. I think those things remind him of Mom. On the other hand, other times he seems fine talking about her, like in connection to dance or those art pieces. I don't know....Anyway, I've grown accustomed to his mood swings and little trances. Don't let it bother you. He snaps out of it pretty quickly."

"I wish I could stay here with you all the time," I said, listening to the pleasant sound of nothing outside.

"Well, I'll be going to school in the city soon, so if you are in New York, I can keep giving you lessons." As optimistic as she was about Gina and Mr. Raider, she knew enough not to encourage me too much so soon.

"But I like it here!" I said, feeling the luxurious sheets and the pillow-top mattress. "I've never had my own room before."

Sam turned my hand over in hers and put our bracelets side to side.

"Well, we can't control that, but no matter what happens between our parents," Sam said, "let's pledge to be sisters forever."

I sat up in bed and threw my arms around Samantha.

"Dad really likes your mom though. I can tell. He's come back to life!"

"How did your Mom die?" I asked.

Sam looked thoughtful for a moment as she considered what would be prudent to say to me at my age.

"Someone killed her. It was awful. That was before we moved here."

"What happened?!"

"Ophelia, I'm not sure this is a topic for bedtime."

"I've seen lots of dead people."

"Please don't ask me anymore right now, Okay, Sis?

"Okay, Sister." I hugged her again.

"Well, if there's anything you need, let me

know," Sam continued. "You can watch TV until you fall asleep."

Though I had just said I wouldn't, I couldn't help but ask, "Do you know why someone would want to kill your mother?"

"I promise you, I don't know," Sam answered. "Now that's *enough*. Wanna see something cool?"

I nodded my head in agreement, as she beckoned me to follow her. Sam brought me to a wall, then pressed a button underneath the lamp that stood beside it. The door slowly crept open exposing a narrow hallway.

"All of the bedrooms have hallways that lead to the panic room. See up there? You can monitor these cameras and others around the house and property from the control room and from within the panic room."

"What's a panic room?" I asked as we entered the newly exposed hallway. The room wasn't as large as the bedroom, but it was comfortable enough, and it was at least as big as the room Mamma and I shared at home.

"You can always feel safe in this house, because we have this amazing hiding place. Dad is overcautious ever since what happened to Mom."

What is better than a mansion? A mansion with a secret room! We were far away from the city, where the scary boys fought and where Sam's mother was murdered. *What could go wrong in this neighborhood and in this house?*

Sam led me back to the bedroom, and I crawled back in bed, pulling the poufy bedspread up to my neck.

"You comfy? Good! And if you don't like being alone, you can come crawl in with me. You want the TV on?"

After a couple of hours, I went downstairs to look for something to snack on. While I stood in front of the refrigerator, Mr. Raider came walking in from his study. He got each of us a glass–water for him, milk for me–and a bowl for snacks. He poured some nuts in his bowl and then walked back out. He hadn't said a single word. After all that Sam has said, I just accepted this as more of Mr. Raider's quirky ways. I went back upstairs to enjoy my very own room, even if it was for just one night. I don't know how long it was before I fell asleep with the television going.

8

THE BLESSINGS OF SHARING

The next morning, I could hardly wake when Sam came to my room around seven. It was time to unclutter Ms. Doyle's house to get her mind right. Sam seemed excited about her important role in the day's activities and gave up on rousing me, but I was soon lured by the smell of bacon and waffles and happy sounds from downstairs.

As I made my way down, I heard the three of them talking about Ms. Doyle, the hoarder and her giant halls of treasures and trash.

"I'm not going to find any dead bodies in there, am I?" Mamma asked Sam.

"If you find a dead *Mr. Doyle*, don't worry, he had it coming," Mr. Raider said wryly. "More likely dead cats. She used to have a lot of pets, but I don't know what happened to them."

I couldn't wait to see this place–but I was a little scared. She sounded like a real witch, the way they were talking.

After breakfast, I sat with Sam while she packed a giant bag. It looked like she was going to beauty school rather than a yard sale. In went hairbrush, curling iron, scissors, hair dryer, piles of makeup, an impressive assortment of brushes, sponges and other things I didn't even recognize. Sam's plan was to give Doyle a makeover, so that she would feel more comfortable about facing the onslaught of customers Sam was expecting. Wisely, Sam suggested we stay behind then join her in an hour at Ms. Doyle's.

When she arrived, the gate didn't swing open automatically for Samantha–it was already open. Ms. Doyle was standing out front, looking like she had been hung up wet to dry. She was shaking with anger.

"Good morning, Ms. Doyle," Sam said in a bright, chipper voice.

"Good morning, my ass!" Doyle answered. "Don't tell me good morning. What's good about it? I have been waiting for you since five o'clock! I don't think I can do this. Not yet. Tell these men to put my stuff back!"

"Take a deep breath, Ms. Doyle," Sam asserted. "We got almost everything done yesterday. You knew this was going to be difficult."

Ms. Doyle appreciated Sam's take-charge attitude. It was what she needed to hear.

"Now, please, Ms. Doyle, go take a shower."

As if by design, Molly arrived just as Ms. Doyle disappeared inside. Sam and Molly walked across the lawn and beheld two large tents that had been erected on it. In order to make the sale look more like a flea market and less like preparations for a bonfire, the movers were taking most of the smaller items from inside the house and arranging them under one tent or the other. For the next forty-five minutes, Sam and Molly made final decisions about the arrangement of the items. Finally we arrived, and Sam introduced everyone to each other before taking Mamma and me inside to meet Ms. Doyle.

Ms. Doyle managed to be polite to Mamma through our introductions, but she couldn't help complaining as Mamma put her hairstyling education to work. Sam and Mamma laughed at the fact that they both came prepared. There was two of practically everything. Ms. Doyle just glared at them as if to say, *If you are going to do this, just do it already!* My job was to clean up her dirty fingernails.

I didn't know yet that I was mostly just dealing with dirt from the garden, and I was pretty grossed out by Ms. Doyle's hands, but Mom kept making me giggle by silently mocking Ms. Doyle's complaints behind her back. A natural-born leader, Sam went out to see if Mr. Raider and Molly needed direction. Soon, Mamma was done giving Ms. Doyle a fierce pixie cut that matched her fiery personality. It was only when she was done styling it that Ms. Doyle started to warm up to us. Despite her reservations, she loved it.

Afterwards, Samantha asked us to join Molly and Mr. Raider on the cleaning squad. Sam then went to work exfoliating a few years off Ms. Doyle. The complaining started up again, but Sam felt comfortable enough with Doyle at this point to respond with good humored teasing.

"Oh, you poor, poor thing getting a facial in your own bathroom. Life is so, so, hard." Then, Sam made up Ms. Doyle's face.

"I can stand to look at myself in the mirror again!" Doyle exclaimed when she saw herself for the first time. She stood there staring at the large hall mirror in the one part of the giant house, other than the kitchen, where nothing was for sale. She never said thank you, but when she reappeared from her bedroom after a couple of minutes of searching, she was carrying three unopened boxes that had postage from Italy. "These are for you," she said, and then went back in the bedroom to get dressed.

It was another trio of packages for this trio who had been brought together by another yard sale not altogether unlike this one. Nothing could have prepared us for what was in those boxes. Although dated from five years before and filled with dust, the outer boxes contained lovely round boxes inside, which in turn contained spectacular hats. The hat was more beautiful than anything else I owned, with the sole exception of the violin Sam had given me. I ran my hand over the silver and gold threading of the hat, having trouble believing it was mine. Mamma threw her hands up in the air when she saw her mint green colored Amy Hamilton Hat.

Ms. Doyle came back in a nice dress with big, geometric blocks of color and said, matter of fact, "Miss Hamilton sent me those hats, but I never had a reason to wear them."

We had turned a switch on in Ms. Doyle, and it looked like nothing could ever turn it off again. She invited us into her closet where she started to show us her collection of high-fashion clothing, shoes, and handbags. We all were blown away by the chatty, stylish person Ms. Doyle had suddenly become. Her closet became a portal into the rarified life of an A-List New Yorker. Molly stuck her head in then, suddenly, we were all playing dress-up with Ms. Doyle insisting on giving us whatever worked best for each of us.

Sam exclaimed, "Now this is what I call quality girl time!"

Molly started doing her best catwalk and singing, *"I'm a model, you know what I mean, and I do my little turn on the catwalk…."*

When Mama did her little turn on the catwalk, I couldn't believe my eyes. Mamma was a *hot* mamma. I felt like my little dance was definitely the best, because it expressed the joy that had been building up inside of me.

Then, Sam starting doing absurd looking modern dance moves in her underwear and hopping all around us. We laughed and laughed.

This went on for about twenty minutes until Sam suddenly became aware of the time and threw on her work clothes. Ms. Doyle had managed to divest herself of many thousands of dollars' worth of clothing, and we didn't mind that a bit. There was still a lot to do and it was getting close to the time of the sale.

Sam assigned us each a task. Mr. Raider and Mamma would be in charge of selling the furniture inside the house. Molly and Sam would each take a tent. I would relay questions to Ms. Doyle about specific items. And Ms. Doyle, to her chagrin, was in charge of greeting everyone and showing hospitality. The salespeople went to their areas to finish arranging things, while Ms. Doyle and I looked for items that didn't have price tags yet.

The first people to arrive through those gates were old friends from the neighborhood of Ms. Doyle whom she had refused to talk to or see for five years. Two of them were women she played golf with every Wednesday at the ritzy country club nearby. After seeing her again for the first time in five years, they wept, each taking a turn holding her tightly. When the clock struck nine, people started to arrive in car loads. Doyle surprised herself by having a very good time, but not a better time than Sam, who reveled in the success of bringing Ms. Doyle out of her shell. Doyle walked around asking people about their interest in particular items and then deciding whether to charge for them or just cut the price further. For the most part, the others just accepted whatever price, the shopper suggested

Two hours later, the new, good old Ms. Doyle was struck with an idea to turn the yard sale into a celebration. She called several restaurants and ordered food to be delivered. Customers helped the team consolidate the few remaining outdoor items under one tent and the tables under the other tent soon displayed a generous and eclectic buffet lunch. Forty people or so, some from the neighborhood, some who traveled for the sale, sat eating together. Doyle let her old friends know how happy she was to reconnect with them on this day, but also told them directly that she was done with golf and other leisure pursuits. She had lived narcissistically long enough, first in business and society, then in solitary gardening. The rest of her life would be devoted to philanthropy.

When she was done eating, she walked over to where Sam was seated and hugged her from behind.

"Thanks for giving me my life back," she said. "I couldn't have done this without you."

Ms. Doyle next delight was to gather all the children who were there for a tour of her greenhouse. The children came out running to find their parents and pulled them back across the lawn. The four hour yard sale turned into a six hour event that brought happiness to everyone involved. We all felt blessed to be there. We suddenly noticed, though, that not everyone had remained. Where were Mamma and Mr. Raider? Gone somewhere together, we presumed. Sam, Molly and I got to work with Ms. Doyle and some of her friends turning the Doyle mansion back into a home.

DIAMONDS & DELIVERANCE

Sam felt like she could do no wrong. Beginning with that first bit of generosity of giving the violin, every bit of goodwill she felt or acted upon seemed to yield immediate benefits. Mamma and Mr. Raider relished each other's company. What was supposed to be a one night's sleepover justified by the yard sale was extended by spontaneous trips to the upper Connecticut and a ferry ride to Fire Island.

Clothes from Ms. Doyle's had Mamma and me fitting right into the upper class crowd with Mr. Raider and Sam–even standing out impressively to the ladies who knew what we were wearing. Wherever we went, I brought my violin and found time to play.

There was some concern Ms. Doyle would backslide emotionally, but Sam skipped the ferry ride to spend the day with her, exchanging ideas about how get her big philanthropic plans off the ground.

Returning to the Bronx after weekending with the upper class was a bit jarring, but by the time the summer was done, we had been treated to so many expensive trips that I was a little burnt out on lavish living and beginning to find a new appreciation for my own neighborhood. It's funny how narrow-minded I had become after having little exposure to anything outside The Bronx. What the Bronx lacked in natural beauty it made up for in cultural density.

And being stuck inside when it wasn't safe to go out, isn't as bad when all I wanted to do was fiddle anyway.

Sam spent the last two weeks of August preparing for school while researching places where Ms. Doyle could make the biggest impact on children's lives. Sam began to convince Ms. Doyle that shipping donated goods around the world might not be the best thing for the environment or people that really needed clean water, education, and food, more than high-fashion clothing and European-style furniture.

Gradually, Sam started to find that her father might be right about whether she could manage both school and Ms. Doyle's project. On orientation day at Juilliard, Sam saw how hard she would have to work to become a world-class dancer who could garner the respect of her peers and instructors. Hearing what some of her classmates had accomplished before getting into Juilliard made her doubt her abilities. She worried people might think she was there because of her mother's reputation, not because of her own form. Her solution? Out-practice the competition.

By the final week in August, only Mr. Raider showed up at our house in the evenings. Sam was taking classes and practicing alone frequently at the most prestigious studio she could find in the city. She knew she needed to get past the "big fish in a little pond" syndrome.

Luckily, Ms. Doyle took up Sam's slack in terms of being supportive to Molly, helping her get her G.E.D and getting her accepted into a college out of town so she could keep her pregnancy unknown in Greenwich. Mamma, already accustomed to commuting to Greenwich for work, now worked for Ms. Doyle on Saturdays cleaning that big house or accompanying her on an occasional errand when Ms. Doyle was not up to going out alone. This meant I got to enjoy my Bronx home during the week and Mr. Raider's every weekend.

There was another reason Sam was never around. She had gotten her wish and had found a boy who was just as obsessed with dancing as she was. Giovanni was an Italian-born twenty year old who had come to Juilliard to pursue a dancing career. They had met briefly during orientation, and then deepened their friendship when he joined the same studio as Sam. One evening, when she had come to the Bronx to give me one of my increasingly rare violin lessons, she confided in Mamma about Giovanni.

"The way he looks at me does something to me that I can't even explain," Sam said. "When we are dancing together it feels like we are one body."

"I don't think you need to explain," Mamma said with a twinkle, but then got serious. "Sounds like a dream, Samantha, but don't move too fast now."

"You mean like you and Dad?"

Mamma smiled, blushed, and looked down.

"I mean, you are lovely and special Sam, and it wouldn't surprise me if he is head over heels over you. But he wouldn't be the first boy to lead a girl on, you know?"

Sam could only nod her head knowing that Mamma spoke the truth. After all, Justin, the town's player, used to be her best friend. "And don't forget," Mama asserted. "Your father and I have been around the block before. Experience counts for something in affairs of the heart. I know when a man is in it only for one thing."

"He hasn't even kissed me, Gina!"

"Well, you better find out if he likes you before you fall any deeper."

"I will," Sam said thoughtfully, "if I can muster the courage."

"Your Dad is on his way," Mamma said. It was Thursday night, which meant dinner in Chinatown. "Samantha, between you and me, do you think that your dad and I are moving too fast?"

"No, I was only teasing you," Sam answered. "I think you guys make a great couple. I have not seen my dad this happy in a long time. I thank God that you're in our lives...Gina, are you okay? Gina, why are you crying?" Sam moved closer to Mamma on the couch and took her hand.

"I don't even know," Mamma answered. "These are happy tears though. I think I'm in love with your dad. I have never been happier with anyone in my entire life. He cares so much for me. I've never had that. I've never had anyone treat me like I deserve respect, comfort, and affection."

"I'm sure Dad feels just as strongly about you, Gina," Samantha answered.

Mamma wiped her tears and turned to me. "Come here little girl," she said with her arms out. "Come hug me."

I ran to her and threw myself in her lap. She hugged me tightly then grabbed Sam and hugged her too.

A sudden car horn startled us. We all knew it was Mr. Raider. None of us were ready for dinner. We all jumped up and quickly changed clothes, bringing makeup and accessories in handbags to put on in the car. Nothing could have prepared us for what Mr. Raider had planned that night. He seemed nervous and out of sorts, especially when he greeted us as we climbed into the car. Twice he almost caused an accident. One time, he had to slam on his breaks to avoid hitting a boy crossing the street."Focus, Dad!" Sam yelled from the back seat. "What's are you thinking man?"

Mr. Raider let out a weird grin but never answered Sam. Mamma asked if he was okay when she noticed he was sweating more than normal after the near miss with the boy.

"Never better," he answered.

This reply didn't help one bit. Everyone was on edge as we drove to the city.

When we arrived in at the restaurant, he stood there talking to the greeter instead of walking to the table with us and pulling out the chairs as he usually did.

"Is everything okay with Martin?" Mamma asked Sam as we found our seats.

"Well, he's up to something. I can tell."

When he finally got to the table, he sat quickly and avoided making eye contact. He ordered food without taking any suggestions and then sat there looking smug, waiting for approval. He was twiddling his thumbs like a mad scientist. We all examined him keenly, and then turned towards each other. Suddenly, we all broke out laughing. When the food arrived, Mr. Raider scarfed it down like it was the first time he had seen food in days.

"I know you love Chinese food, but don't choke," Sam said.

"Are you high on something, Martin?" Mamma chimed in. "You look like you are coming out of a drug binge. You're eating so fast.

He was finished with his dinner well before the rest of us. He just sat there looking impatient as we finished our food. It had become a ritual for us to read and discuss our fortune cookies every Thursday. Mr. Raider's, Sam's, and my fortunes all promised us a prosperous future. We were ooh-ing and ah-ing by the time it was Mamma's turn. When Mamma broke her cookie, a diamond ring fell out on the table. The look on her face was priceless! She picked up the ring then looked animatedly at all of us. Mr. Raider pushed back his chair, positioned himself in front of hers, and then knelt down.

"Gina, will you marry me?"

I felt previledged to witness the proposal. My mother screamed like a young girl, something I would never have expected from her under any circumstance. Everyone in the restaurant clapped, especially the staff who had helped Mr. Raider arrange his proposal. Her screams were followed by tears, then a huge embrace.

"Yes, Martin. Yes yes yes yes yes." She may have cut off the circulation to Mr. Raider's brain because he was looking rather dazed by the time she let go of him.

"I'm finally going to have a sister!" Sam said, and I looked over to see her coming at me with open arms.

When Mr. Raider finally pulled himself together, he gave me a hug and said, "I have a ring for you too, Ophelia."

He then handed me the little black box. The clustered diamond ring was spectacular and bright, just like my future, I was sure, now, this was my family.

10

THE SHOTGUN WEDDING

Focused on romance by the gesture of love she had seen the day before, Sam went to school the next day thinking hard about Mamma's warnings. After an hour of dancing with Giovanni, she had built up the nerve to take Mamma's advice and make the boy clarify things. In the middle of the dance floor, when the music stopped, he was still holding her. When she looked at him, he was already staring into her deep blue eyes.

"Why do you look at me in that way?" Sam asked Giovanni.

"How do I look at you?"

Sam paused and took a step back from him.

"You know," she continued. "Like you want me."

"I'm just staying in the moment. Dancing is just acting with your whole body."

Clever as that was, it was not what she wanted to hear. "I'm sorry. I just thought." She couldn't finish her statement for fear she would be rejected. She turned to escape into the women's locker room, but suddenly, Giovanni grabbed her by the hand, spun her around, leaned her backwards in his arms, and kissed her.

"I do want you," Giovanni whispered. "The way I look at you is real."

It was Sam's first kiss, and she was hungry for more. Without thinking, she grabbed him, pulled his body against hers and pressed her mouth against his in a deeper, longer kiss. When the kiss finally ended, she once again became self-aware. Embarrassed at how voraciously she had kissed him, Sam grabbed her things and ran out of the studio. She was restless that evening, wondering if her eagerness was too much for him.

The next day, when Sam arrived to the studio, Giovanni presented her with a rose. After the way she had acted, she was grateful for the gesture. They began to dance, and the rose became a prop as they improvised their moves. She glided around the room in a figure eight and handed him the rose. He danced with strong leaps and returned it to her. Back and forth the rose went as they celebrated their art. Sam loved how he reacted to her postures and challenged him to invent new combinations of movement. Sam had a smooth dancer to share her first experience of love with.

My love also grew leaps and bounds, but not for a boy. My romance was with the violin. It had brought so much love, security, and happiness to my life, not to mention the focus and discipline I was developing.

The first day of school, I had only one goal–to join the school orchestra. As soon as recess started, I ran towards the music teacher, interrupting her lunch to inquire how to join.

"Slow down, sweetie," Ms. Scholman said. "You are gonna hyperventilate, talking so fast."

I did my best to speak slowly. "My name is Ophelia. I want to join the orchestra."

"We don't have enough instruments for everyone," she said. "You would have had to reserve your instrument on orientation day two weeks ago. I'm sorry, sweetie."

"I have an instrument," I quickly answered. "I have my violin."

"Wonderful! We need a violinist. Can you play?"

"Somewhat," I answered, unsure as to her standards or my skill level.

"Well, you have a violin, so you must know something," she said.

She was a six-foot tall, full-figured German woman with little glasses set on the edge of her nose. Seeing her walk in the halls, I had assumed she would be stern and have a great, booming voice. I was pleasantly surprised by her bubbly and welcoming personality.

In her soothing voice, she said, "Bring your violin tomorrow during lunch and let me hear you play for a minute.

The next day when I played for her, she asked me how long I had been at it.

"My Mamma found this violin for me at a garage sale last month. My new sister has given me a few lessons, and I play every day."

"What happened to your old violin?"

"I never played before I got this one."

Ms. Scholman looked astonished, as if I had told her she had just won the lottery.

"You're my first prodigy," she exclaimed as she clapped her hands. "You make sure you show up every practice, and if you ever want any new sheet music or extra direction, I have more free time on Fridays."

I didn't know the word "prodigy," but I knew from how she said it, I knew it was good. It was the confirmation I was seeking. It was then I knew that practicing wasn't just fun. I knew I had talent, I wanted to be *the best.* When I arrived home, I told my mother what Ms. Scholman said, she reveled in the compliment, calling her mother and sister to tell them the news. She seemed just as excited to tell them about my talent as she was to tell them she was coming to the Dominican Republic to introduce her fiancé to them.

Yes, I was about to return to the homeland of my mother for a weekend visit at the end of the month with Sam and Mr. Raider. Everything was moving in a good direction for us. Three months before, Mamma was unhappy, and I was bored most days. By then, we bounced out of bed eager to see what each new day would bring.

I remember before, hearing Mamma cry on the phone to her mother, asking her what she had done for God to make her life so bad. Her mother told her she was going to pray and ask God to send her a miracle. It seemed that God was listening, and her mother made sure to remind her that it was Him that brought on all of these wonderful changes. After the phone call that day, Mamma asked Mr. Raider to bring her to Church that Sunday to hear the word of God and thank Him for all that he had done for her. That was one of the things that Mr. Raider had Mamma had in common. They both had a bipolar relationship with God. Both had turned their backs on him after they lost their significant others and had started to praise him since they found each other. As promised to her mother, Mamma made it to church that Sunday with Mr. Raider and me in tow.

After church, Mamma and Mr. Raider decided they didn't want to wait to be married. They decided to marry in the Dominican Republic on the Sunday of their visit. There was no one happier than her mother,

Lupita. None of my mother's family had visas to travel to the United States, so all of them were going to miss her wedding until that decision was made. After years of struggle, Grandma Lupita had sent her daughter off to Mamma's father in the United States. Because Mamma overstayed her visa, she had to wait ten years before she could see her mother again. At the time of her return, I was only three years old, and Mamma had fallen on her own hard times. After she found the job in Greenwich Mamma sent what money she could back to Grandma Lupita, but it wasn't much.

Mamma had taken me to the Dominican Republic before, but those two visits had not been as glorious as the seaside wedding that Mamma and Mr. Raider were planning with Grandma Lupita's help. Mr. Raider wired $30,000 to Grandma for the wedding. That was more money that she had earned in her entire life. Needless to say, Grandma Lupita was quite impressed by Mr. Raider before she even met him. Mamma invited four of her friends and her estranged father to travel to the wedding and all accepted after Mr. Raider insisted on paying their way. Everyone was impressed by him but none more than me. He made my mother happy, and not just by paying for everything and buying her gifts. He demonstrated his care for her by sitting and talking with her for hours, which she adored.

Two weeks before the wedding, Mr. Raider suggested that she quit her job as a housekeeper and figure out what she wanted to do with the rest of her life. Mamma told him she always wanted to own her own hair salon. They both started to scout for a prime location in Portchester for the salon. A week before we left, we started to pack our belongings to move to Greenwich with Mr. Raider. It's not like we had much to carry. Mamma told her friends they could have practically everything in the apartment. The Thursday before we left for the Dominican Republic, instead of going to Chinatown, we packed our clothes, pictures, gifts from Mr. Raider, and my violin, and said goodbye to our little apartment in the Bronx. For me, it was bittersweet, but Mamma was ready to get out of there.

The first night we arrived to our new home, Sam brought Giovanni to Greenwich and introduced him to us. Although her father, being overprotective, was less than thrilled, Sam reminded him that she was a mature girl who made good decisions and had never gotten in trouble. Mr. Raider tried to act as carefree about it, but as soon as Sam stepped out of the room, he pulled Giovanni aside and warned him.

"You take good care of my little girl or I will make sure that the rest of your life is a living hell."

It was a threat, but to Mr. Raider, it was more like a plea for Giovanni to do the right thing and honor Sam. Giovanni promised him he would do just that—of course, he would never let any harm come to Sam.

Sam and Giovanni also paid a visit that same night to Ms. Doyle. When Sam introduced Giovanni to Ms. Doyle, she found out that Ms. Doyle was fluent in Italian and that Doyle's ex-husband was a famous Italian apparel designer who Giovanni knew and probably everyone in Italy was aware of. After a long conversation in Italian, Sam finally interrupted them.

"Hello. I'm here too, you know." she said.

"Excuse me Sam," Ms. Doyle said. "It's been a long time since I've been able to speak Italian. So…are you two dating or just school mates?"

Sam and Giovanni shared a smile.

"I guess we are dating," Sam said coyly.

"Well hang on to this one," Ms. Doyle said. "Giovanni is from the good part of Italy, where boys treat girls like ladies."

"How are you?" Sam asked, trying to change the subject.

"I'm doing very well, thanks to you," she answered. "Molly has been coming here daily. She's a sweetheart, but Justin is making her very unhappy."

"What is he doing?" Sam asked.

"He keeps begging her to have an abortion and threatening her," Ms. Doyle said. "I told her not to worry and that as soon as he sees the baby he will have a change of heart."

Samantha grabbed her phone and dialed Justin's number, while Ms. Doyle talked to Giovanni about her many visits to his country. After a few rings, Justin answered

"You continue to disappoint me," Sam said. '"I would've never thought you could stoop so low as to threaten Molly."

"I'm just afraid of my dad," he said. "I didn't mean to threaten her. Please, Sam, encourage her to have an abortion."

"Look, whether you like it or not, she is going to have this baby. She has plenty of support from us and will be okay without your help. Your father will never know unless you want him to know. Tell him when you see fit, but never threaten Molly again. You hear me?"

Justin agreed and made it clear he was going to stay away from Molly. Sam hung up the phone and gave Ms. Doyle a look of satisfaction, and in turn, she looked back at her with admiration.

"Oh, I forgot to tell you–Molly got into the university," Doyle said. "She'll start in the spring. I told her she can stay here whenever she pleases. I love her company, especially now that you're gone"

"That's so sweet of you, Ms. Doyle," Sam said. "I'm so glad you've opened your house and heart to her."

"So, did you just come over to show off your Italian stud to me or are you here to discuss my philanthropic project?"

"I'm actually here to see you. I wanted to ask you if you will take an impromptu trip to Dominican Republic with us. Dad and Gina are getting married, and I wanted you to be there."

Ms. Doyle was humbled by Sam wanting her to be there and could not turn down the request.

"I'll pack my bags and book a flight if you promise not to ditch me and hang out all the time with your *new mother*. I think Gina is so awesome. We'll have fun!"

Samantha gave Ms. Doyle the information who then called the airline, hoping they could all travel on the same Friday morning flight. Sam left Ms. Doyle in ecstatic anticipation about her first travel in five years. Sam and Giovanni grabbed a quick bite before she dropped him off at the station for his train back to the city. After some shopping for the trip, Sam pulled her green duffel bag from the top of her closet. The packing was interrupted by a late night visit by three men. When Mr. Raider opened the door and saw them standing there in black suits, he immediately closed the door behind himself and walked out to the edge of the porch with them.

Samantha, Mamma, and I could not hear what was being said on the porch, but it was obvious to all of us Mr. Raider was rattled. He came back inside, sweating profusely and could hardly talk when Sam asked him who the men were.

"They're nobody," he answered brusquely and walked through the living room past us where we were helping Mamma pack. We were surrounded by the many bags of goods Mamma had bought to bring with her to DR.

"But I recognize one of those men," Sam exclaimed. "He was there when Mom died!"

Mr. Raider stopped in his tracks and turned to Sam with a bewildered look on his face. He just stood there, staring at her.

"What's going on Martin?" Mamma asked. "Who are those men?"

Realizing that he had to give an answer, Mr. Raider removed his sport jacket, which revealed a light blue polo shirt soaked with sweat. He draped the jacked over the back of a chair and sat down slowly, steeling himself.

"They're from the FBI," he said. "They just found some new information about Caroline's death."

"Did they found out who did it, Daddy?" Sam blurted. "Did they?

"No, but they have a lead," he answered.

Suddenly, Mr. Raider jumped from his chair and rushed to the bathroom. Soon after, we heard him vomiting. Mamma rushed to the door and knocked on it, demanding he open the door. Even at twelve, I knew that Mr. Raider wasn't being forthcoming about why the men were there. They heard the water running and the toilet flush before he opened the door.

"Please tell me what's going on, Martin? Please tell me," Mamma begged.

"Nothing, Babe," he answered. "I just had a flashback, that's all. I'll be okay!" he said convincingly. "Ready for a great wedding?"

"Yes!" Mamma exclaimed and hurried back over to the bags she was packing. "I can't wait to see my Mamma Lupita either."

I realized that my mother's judgment was being clouded by her emotions, but that all changed by the time I went to tell her goodnight in her bedroom. I found her with the lights off, staring out the window. When I called out to her, she became startled and immediately turned to walk towards me. She pulled me into her bedroom and closed the door behind her.

"Those men are still parked outside the house, Ophelia," she whispered. "Why would they be parked outside the house at eleven at night? There is something going on here. Cops only stay at people's houses for two reasons–either they are staking it out, or they're trying to protect the people inside it."

While Mamma's words registered in my mind, I started to recall the panic room that Sam had shown me two months before. I figured it was a good time to let Mamma in on the secret.

"Well, I guess they must be there for a reason, Mamma, and I think Mr. Raider knows why they're here," I said. "But if anyone ever coming for us we can always run to the panic room."

"Panic room?"

"Samantha showed me a large room that is connected to all the bedrooms," I said. "No one will find you once you close yourself in there. You wanna see it?"

A sudden knock at the door startled both of us. Mamma jumped into bed like a gazelle being chased and covered herself as the door opened. I stood there not knowing what to do as Mr. Raider poked his head in.

"I just came to kiss you goodnight," he said.

"Oh, Ophelia came to do the same," Mamma said.

I caught on quickly, walked over to Mamma, kissed her on the cheek and walked out.

I walked to my room but then decided to walk over to Samantha's room to see how she felt about the three men sitting outside our house. Tired from her long day, Sam was sound asleep. When I tried to nudge her awake, she flailed her hands around like she was dancing and fell back asleep.

As I left Sam's room, I could hear Mr. Raider's bedroom door shut at the end of the hallway. Usually, he would've sat in the study downstairs for hours before he went to bed, but not that night. As I was walking back into my bedroom, I saw Mamma tip-toeing out of her bedroom towards me. Closing the door behind us in my room, I made my way over to the secret door of the panic room and pressed the button under the lamp. An amazed and worried look crossed Mamma's face as the hallway and then the panic room lit up on their own. Mamma placed her hands on her hips as she stood there in front of the eight monitors all lit up, showing pictures of every part of the house.

"Andeldiablo. I've never even seen the cameras," Mamma whispered. "This was built for a reason."

"What reason Mamma?" I asked.

"To protect Sam and him from whatever he's hiding from us," she answered.

Mamma kept shaking her head from side to side repeating the same words. "This is not good."

Mamma walked up to each door that led to each bedroom and the bathroom, looking for the one that led to Mr. Raider room.

I could tell she was about to start yelling. I almost tripped over my own two feet rushing over to grab her from behind.

"Mamma, if Samantha finds out that I told you, she will never trust me again," I whispered. "Please don't do this."

"I'm leaving for my wedding to this man tomorrow, and you're worried about some childish pact you made with Sam?"

"Please Mamma," I begged. "Don't ruin our new life!" Mamma knew exactly the situation we were in. She saw the look on my face. We had been living through drive-by-shootings, warring gangs, and the occasional dead body in front of our building in the Bronx.

I missed home a little bit, but I certainly didn't miss my mother's misery.

"Whatever's going on, I'm sure it isn't as bad as you think!"

I was sure we could live with anything if we could avoid going back to the way things were.

"Get me out of here," Mamma said as she walked towards the door, looking for a way out. "I won't say anything, but if Sam tells you anything else or if you hear anything, better let me know."

"I will tell you, Mamma," I promised as we made our way through the door and closed it.

"Don't worry," Mamma said as she kissed me on the cheek. "I'll get to the bottom of this after we arrive back from DR."

Mamma's reassurance helped me to fall asleep that night. I wanted nothing to spoil the weekend she had been looking forward to so much. I awoke the next morning to my mother talking in Spanish loudly. If she wasn't talking to her family, Mamma speaking her native tongue meant trouble. I jumped up and walked to the door and found her standing in the hallway with Mr. Raider. Sam came running out of her bedroom also after she heard the uproar.

"Those men were sitting there the entire night, and they're still outside, Martin!" Mamma yelled.

"Ha...Wha...The men from last night are still there?" Sam chimed, still rubbing her eyes trying to pry them open.

"Yes, and your father refuses to tell me why!" Mamma yelled as she turned towards Samantha. "He must think I'm stupid or something."

"I don't think you're stupid, Gina," Mr. Raider answered. "They must have spent the night there because it was too late to drive back to where they came from."

Mamma had it. She started talking in Spanish again as she made her way down the steps and toward the front door. We all followed behind her. She flung the front door open and marched past the gate to the black car with tinted windows parked across the street.

"Since you won't tell me, I'll ask them myself!" Mamma fumed.

Mr. Raider started running after her, but he was too late. As she knocked on the roof of the car, the back window rolled down slowly.

"Why are you camping out here?" Mamma asked. "I'm going to marry this man on Sunday, and he has refused to tell me why three men from the FBI are sitting outside the house I'm supposed to live in with my daughter." The driver's door came open, and a tall white man in his thirties climbed out of the sedan.

"Calm down, ma'am," he said. "I understand your concern, but I can assure you we're here for a good reason."

"And what is that reason?" Mamma asked as Mr. Raider tried to pull her back. "What is the reason?!" she yelled.

The man looked Mamma in the eyes with sympathy, then at Sam and me standing on the front porch, then at Mr. Raider.

"I think you owe them the truth, Martin," the man said, then opened the car door and took his seat.

Mr. Raider held Mamma by the hand.

"I will tell you Gina," he said. "Let's just go in the house and put some clothes on."

Mamma had forgotten that she was wearing a revealing nightgown. She grabbed her hand away from Mr. Raider, tugged her nightgown shut then made her way past us towards the front door. Sam demanded that her father tell the truth when Mamma and her Dad walked past us on the porch.

"Tell me now or else the wedding is off," Mamma blurted. "Now!"

Mr. Raider sat on the couch, leaned forward, forearms on his knees.

"They think the same man who killed Caroline wants to kill me too," he said.

All three of us sat there without uttering one word. We couldn't. Mamma looked at him closely, reading his expression, trying to determine whether he was telling the truth.

"I don't think he will ever find me," Mr. Raider continued.

"Why, Dad?" Sam said. "Why did he kill Mom, and why would he still be after you?"

"I don't know," he answered. "But I don't think he will ever find me."

"Those men would not be outside your damn house, Martin, if they thought he couldn't find you,"

Mamma stated. "But why now? Why after all this time, would he want to find you?"

"I don't know," Mr. Raider muttered. "I will protect us. I'll find a couple of bodyguards when we arrive back home, and those agents will probably follow us all the way to the airport."

"There must be a reason," Sam said. "There must be a reason why he would kill Mom and come after you. Dad you need to be honest and tell us the whole story. I swear I won't get mad!"

Sam's plea made her father become very emotional. As tears ran down his face, he started to talk, barely getting the words out.

"I swear I didn't know Samantha," he cried. "I swear I didn't know they would come after us."

He immediately wiped his tears, realizing that he had just admitted knowing who killed Sam's mother and why.

"They were my business partners," he said. "They were unhappy that I went to the cops and reported their actions."

Sam stood there in shock and kept staring at him.

"All this time," she said, shaking her head. "You knew. You knew who did it. You knew all this time."

Sam turned and stormed up the stairs towards the bedroom and slammed the door. Mr. Raider jumped to follow her.

"Let her calm down, Martin," Mamma said. "Why did you feel like you couldn't confide in me about this?"

He turned towards Mamma and walked back over towards her.

"I figured you would run for sure," he said. "I was afraid of losing you. I'm sorry."

"We can deal with this, but you're hiding things from me that can affect our family–that I can't live with."

"Please don't leave me," Mr. Raider said. "I'm in love with you. I need you. I would never let any harm come to you or the girls. I swear to you, I will protect our family."

"You better!"

Mr. Raider walked over to where Mamma sat and threw himself on the ground in front of her, then placed his head in her lap. Signaling her forgiveness, she began to stroke his head.

I was relieved! Still concerned about Sam, however, I walked up the stairs and knocked on her bedroom door. I tried the handle, but the door was locked. After I called her name four times, she finally and opened the door, slumped back into bed, then pulled the sheets all the way, covering her face.

I didn't know what to do or say. The only thing I could think of was to show her that I loved her. Seeing my new sister sad made me sad as well. I climbed in bed and held her like I was her Mamma. Soon, though, Sam had pulled herself together and turned to trying to comfort me.

"Daddy is a good man. He would never try to hurt anyone. You know about the panic room, the extreme precautions he has taken. Now we know why."

I had seen this man at is best, and now I had seen him at his worst. I believed deeply in my heart he would be a good husband to my mother and a good father to me.

"Is your mom still going to marry my dad?" Sam asked.

"She will," I answered. "She loves him and wouldn't leave at the first sign of trouble. Trust me, we've seen trouble up close and personal. While this is serious, it seems unreal in comparison."

As soon as I finished my sentence, Sam's door slowly opened. Mr. Raider and Mamma came into the room. He apologized to Sam, while Mamma begged her to come to the wedding after she told them she didn't want to attend.

"I don't want your apologies, Dad," Sam yelled after the fifth apology. "I want you to find my mom's killer and make sure he pays for taking her away from me."

"I promise, I'll get to the bottom of this, Sam," Mr. Raider said. "I swear on your mother's grave."

A phone call from Ms. Doyle, who wondered who was coming to drive her to the airport, was enough to make all of us spring into action. After an hour packing the rest of Mamma's wedding stuff and loading everything into Mr. Raider's and Sam's cars, we picked up Ms. Doyle. She was waiting on her front porch, ready to go.

When Mr. Raider saw Ms. Doyle's three large vintage suitcases that looked like something from the thirties, he said exaggeratedly, "uh oh." We all broke out laughing, relieved to let out a little stress. Before long, Mr. Raider was trying to squish Sam's green duffel bag in the little space behind the back headrests of Sam's car.

"You are wrinkling everything!"

Given his obsessive tendencies, Mr. Raider refused to admit defeat in this packing puzzle challenge. He was even more concerned about making Ms. Doyle upset, so he agreed to let her call a taxi to carry some of the luggage. Sam drove me and Ms. Doyle in her car while my Mr. Raider drove Mamma in his.

After minutes passed, Ms. Doyle reached over from the passenger's seat and waved her hand in front of Sam's face.

"Do you have a policy of silence while driving?" Ms. Doyle joked. There was no music going and Sam had been stone-faced the entire trip.

"Want to talk about it?" Doyle asked. "Are you feeling a little jealous at the thought of sharing your dad? That would be understandable. Nothing wrong with talking about your feelings. You taught me that."

Sam laughed with Ms. Doyle, the first time since the night before.

"No," Sam said. "It's been an eye opening twenty four hours, that's all."

"I just saw you last night, and you were fine."

"Well, a lot can happen overnight," Sam said. "I'll be okay."

"You're sure? Because I need you to be on alert, making sure you take good care of me on this trip. Don't worry, in four hours we'll be sipping margaritas by the Caribbean Sea." Ms. Doyle said. "Not you, Ophelia. Don't even think about it," she added, teasingly.

It wasn't long before we had to tell Ms. Doyle what was bothering us. "Why do you keep checking your mirror?" she asked.

"They're still following us."

Ms. Doyle twisted to look out the back window at the black sedan. "Who?"

"FBI agents." Sam said.

Sam explained what she had discovered. Ms. Doyle welcomed the escort after Sam caught her up. The mood remained somber until we ran into Mamma's friends at the ticketing counter. Their screams of excitement changed our moods for the better immediately. Soon, everyone was happy we were on our way to a joyous occasion. I was still nervous, but I had more to be happy about than to worry about so I let go.

Sam and I stopped in the store and bought music and snacks, while Mamma and her friends quickly grabbed food and cocktails from a bar near the boarding gate. As we boarded the plane it appeared as if all was back to normal. It wasn't long before the three-hour plane ride turned ruckus once the flight attendants started serving alcohol to the adults. When we arrived in DR they were intoxicated.

Mr. Raider handled it well when Mamma warned him not to embarrass her in front of her family, especially her mother. Seeing Grandma Lupita for the first time in four years was a treat for me. The little woman with a larger than life personality had tears in her eyes as she looked at me from head to toe. She didn't know one word of English, and my Spanish was poor at best, since Mamma had a policy of sticking to English when possible in order to master the language. As Grandma fired off words to us, Mamma kept translating everything in English while hugging all of her family members.

After the sixth hug, I stopped keeping track of all the people who were hugging me. The entire family seemed to be there at the airport, or so I thought until we reached the Casa De Campo Resort. Grandma had used Mr. Raider's money to rent the entire hotel! What was originally planned as a small wedding reception was to be attended by over two hundred family members.

We drove to the resort to find our rooms. Then, a group of us loaded into a charter bus to get to the rehearsal. The large Catholic Church was fit for the wedding of a princess. I basked in the happiness of my mother, who was grateful that she finally was going to have the kind of wedding she had dreamt of since she was a girl my age.

The rehearsal ran long, so we went directly to the beach party that had been arranged without having a chance to change into beach attire. The church had been so hot and we were so elated–a bunch of us jumped into the Caribbean Sea with all our clothes on! The party raged on through the night, with music blasting from loud speakers and men and women prancing around like it was their last night on this earth.

The alcohol flowed and soon the entire beach became like one big bachelor and bachelorette party. Ms. Doyle's once reserved and withdrawn personality gave way to that of a raunchy hedonist. Soon, she had three men grinding and groping her as she danced the evening away on the beach.

For a while, I sat there and watched everyone lose their inhibitions, freeing themselves of their worldly cares. Mr. Raider and Mamma soon looked like two college kids at a Daytona Beach Spring Break instead of two grownups getting married the next day. Grandma Lupita, the dedicated Christian, sat back and got drunk. She was never judgmental in the slightest, which made me love her even more.

Sam never drank too much, but after two margaritas, she joined the party and danced for hours, letting go of her anger. Several young boys asked me to dance. But at third offer, when Grandma Lupita nudged me and looked at me as if I was being rude, I danced to a couple of songs. It was my first time dancing with a boy. He was very polite and held my hand, showing me all the dance moves that every local man seemed to have mastered.

As the songs played on, all I could think about was making my own music. I felt compelled to return to the hotel room, where I sat and played the violin for hours. It wasn't long before I fell asleep then woke up to the blinding sun in my face. Jumping out of bed to close the blinds, I noticed Sam sprawled out in the other queen bed, wearing the same clothes she had arrived in.

11

BLOWBACK

After a large buffet breakfast filled with local foods like plantains and *yucca* yams, we all arrived at the 1:00 p.m. service. Most of the locals had recovered from their drunkenness, but the visitors to DR, like Ms. Doyle, were still hung over. Wearing sunglasses to block their bloodshot eyes, they dragged themselves into the church like they were attending a funeral.

Being the flower girl, I walked in front of my mother as she approached Mr. Raider, who waited at the altar for his beautiful bride. He looked handsome and dapper, and Mamma looked absolutely stunning. Mamma's friends from back home were her bridesmaids, while Mamma's brother and two cousins served as groomsmen. Sam and Ms. Doyle were seated in the front row on one side, Grandma Lupita and her three sisters, along with hundreds of family members on the other. It looked like the huge church might tip to one side, because the bride's outweighed the groom's. The priest started to talk as Mamma and Martin joined hands together at the altar. We knew the couple was nervous, but from our seats, they looked like the happiest people on earth.

Less than a minute into the prayers to bless the ceremony, gunfire echoed in the domed church.

Being so accustomed to the sound, I barely flinched. I thought I was in some type of dream for a minute because gunfire was so unexpected in the context of a church. Then, I looked around me and saw everyone cowering in their seats and knew something was terribly wrong.

Six gunmen barged into the church with large automatic weapons and demanded that everyone stay still. The men surrounded everyone, and then a tall black man, wearing camouflaged attire, toting a machete, came walking in behind them. He walked straight up to the altar, then leaned the machete strategically on the large cross at the altar. The priest stepped towards him bravely and demanded to know why they brought weapons into the house of God. The man took out a pistol and commanded that the priest kneel down and ask God to spare his life. The priest kneeled but attempted to maintain his dignity by keeping his head upright. The man grabbed the microphone and looked at my mother and Martin, who were still there holding each other's hands, and started to talk.

"Do you know who this man is that you're marrying?" the man said in an African accent I had heard before while visiting Harlem to have my hair braided. "His real name is Jerry La Roche."

Mamma immediately looked at Mr. Raider in shock. She realized the men were here for her fiancé. One of the men set up a video camera in the aisle and started to film everything.

The man started to talk as if he was a preacher, enunciating and emphasizing every word he uttered.

"This man is a criminal who caused the death of ten thousand men, women, and children in Darfur. This man is guilty of financing genocide against my people. Eight years ago, when the government of Darfur started to kill their own people, the United Nations sanctioned the government by banning anyone from conducting business with it. Without funds, the government's atrocities would slow down greatly. However, Mr. La Roche, here, who was the head of his bank, and some of his colleagues, decided that they were going to profit off the genocide by buying the oil reserves that belonged to the people of Darfur. The government used that money to fund more killing. They came to my village and murdered everyone. I watched the decapitation of my own wife and two daughters."

The man paused, while he pulled his long machete out of its sheath. He looked at my mother. Silence permeated the church until the man held the machete up to my mother's throat. There was a whimper from the congregation.

"We killed your last wife, and now you have another beautiful lady here, Mr. La Roche. What do you have to say for yourself, Mr. La Roche?"

"Please don't hurt her," he said. "She had nothing to do with it. I just met her."

"Oh, I know you just met her. You thought you were safe because you changed your name. It slowed us down, but we already had your financial information. I had my people watch your accounts, waiting for you to use them in a traceable way. We waited five years, until finally you sent the wire transfer to your bride's mother.

He then turned to my mother and commanded her to "kneel down," while pushing her down from behind.

When Mamma fell to the ground, her two brothers and five of her cousins rushed towards the man. The armed men opened fire, killing two of them on the spot. Everyone began to scream and moan. The devil walked. I saw my mother on the floor and, although I wanted to rush to her, my body was frozen with fear. The rest of the men let go after two more soldiers pulled out machetes and started to chop up my uncles. Blood was everywhere. Screams turned to tears and pleading.

Suddenly, the man started to yell over the microphone. "We are not here for you, but if anyone else tries to be a hero, we are going to kill everyone in this church!"

He then turned his pistol toward one of the men who had grabbed him and shot him five times.

"Now where were we," he continued. "I'm going to behead your wife as you caused my wife to be beheaded. You will watch helplessly… as I did."

The man picked up the machete and circled to the back of my mother. One huge swipe at Mamma's neck and her head went flying from her body. Her head rolled down the altar in front of everyone in the church. Her body fell slumped to the ground before Mr. Raider. My mind couldn't grasp what I was seeing. I walked slowly towards my mother's head, picked it up, and started walking towards her corpse. Martin, who had begged for mercy before the beheading, now grew infuriated, screaming, rose to his knees, and lunged at the man wielding the machete. The man quickly pulled his pistol from his waist and shot Martin in his kneecap.

"You don't need that leg anymore," the man said. "You know, a lot of our children were maimed because of you. They still drag themselves around the village to this day."

He walked over to Martin, who was now on his back, grabbing his left knee in agony, and chopped his right leg off with two hard swipes of the machete. The terrorist seemed to be having fun as he swiped off Martin's other leg.

Ms. Doyle had pushed Sam under the bench she sat on, but when Sam heard the screaming, she tried to run to help her father.

"They're going to kill you too," Ms. Doyle whispered. "Stay where you are."

"Don't worry, we're not going to kill you," the man said to Mr. Raider. "Killing you would put you out of your misery. You will stay alive, knowing you are responsible for the death of your loved ones."

The man turned towards Mr. Raider and unleashed another blow before throwing the machete aside. He then picked up Mr. Raider's severed right hand, the microphone and walked up to the camera.

"Thieves got their right hand chopped off in the Bible," he said as he dangled the hand around. "Let this be a lesson to all who profited from the genocides in Africa. We are coming for you and your family"

The men all walked out of the church carrying Mr. Raider's severed legs and hand like trophies. As soon as they walked out, some people rushed out of the church, while others rushed to the altar to help Mr. Raider and the others who were hurt. I was crying over my mother's body until Ms. Doyle came and pulled me away. I became inconsolable and screamed for them to let me return to my mother's side.

I screamed for hours until I was sedated.

In the following days, there were times where I couldn't move. I kept thinking how good things were only days before the traumatic event. My mother's gruesome slaughter continually replayed in my head.

I had enough sense to know that Sam could also have been a complete wreck, but when she greeted me with a hug and began talking, she seemed strong and in control of her emotions.

"Ophelia, words cannot describe the pain I feel," she said. "Words cannot describe how sorry I am that this happened because of what my father did. I don't even know how to start to make this right."

Her father was responsible for both our mothers' deaths. It was saying this fact out loud that made her emotional. Her presence reminded me of the times while playing the violin. I retrieved it and began to play, hoping it would bring us some comfort. It did not. It was the violin that brought us all together. My Mamma would still be alive it weren't for this violin.

I threw it to the floor where I stood. My body buckled under its own weight as my mind remembered that the person who I loved the most in this world was gone. Sam came and hugged me from behind as I started to bawl again. For the next twenty four hours, I cried. Ms. Doyle kept close watch over me and Sam the entire time. She kept reminding me that my mother would have wanted me to be strong and get through this. Grandma Lupita came for two hours to sit with me, then told us she was preparing my mother's funeral. The only time we left the hotel Monday was for Ms. Doyle went to the local bank pick up money wired in to cover Mamma's funeral. Sam reluctantly visited her father in the hospital during that time.

I never even thought about his suffering once. As far as I was concerned, he was the reason why my mother was butchered. I wasn't the only one that felt that way. Sam wanted nothing to do with her father, but Ms. Doyle said we should leave judgment for God. I could not understand or accept that concept at that time. Maybe I was too young. Maybe I was too hurt.

When Sam arrived at the hospital, she was mobbed by a score of reporters from every news channel in the United States. They all wanted a piece of the story of a woman dying on her wedding day. Sam never stopped to talk and tried to hide her face by pulling her sweater over her head, but the story was already out that she was Mr. Raider's daughter and that she had survived the attack by hiding under the benches. Sam walked into the hospital room and was immediately asked to give blood for her father by the attending nurse. After agreeing to do it, she walked over to his bedside and looked at him wrapped up in bandages. He was full of drugs but alert.

"I came here to say goodbye," Sam disclosed as she looked down at her fingers. She then looked her father in the eye and said, "I don't ever want to see you again. You've been lying to me for so long and now another person is dead because of your horrible deeds. You repulse me. I don't even know who you are. How could you? You knew! How could you let Gina die like that because of your selfishness? You knew the entire time."

Tears came to Mr. Raider's eyes. He then looked away to the window beside his bed without ever talking.

"Just like I thought," Sam continued. "You have nothing to say, just like when I asked you what happened to Mom. Did Mom know what you did before she died? Did she?"

"She found out when the FBI confronted me about it," he babbled. "She demanded that I return all the money and make reparations, but by then, it was too late."

"Mom would never spend that disgusting blood money," Sam said. "And I won't either. I don't even know who you are. You're a monster! Don't ever contact me."

As Sam turned away walked out of the room, the nurse reminded her about giving blood.

"I'm not giving anything to him," she yelled and kept walking. She could hear her father calling her name in the background, but Sam never answered. Sam walked out of the hospital and stood there in front of the many reporters, who barraged her with questions.

"I just have one thing to say," she paused. "My father is a repulsive animal who deserved what he had coming to him. I am deeply sorry it cost other good people their lives as well."

Sam walked to our waiting taxi and directed the driver to take us to the hotel. Ms. Doyle became livid, demanding Sam to tell her why she would announce that she is the daughter of Mr. Raider. Sam nonchalantly answered that she didn't care if she died. She made it clear she was having a hard time living with what happened. Ms. Doyle finally let up after she realized that Sam could very well be suicidal. Doyle did everything she could to keep us calm. She even hired a psychologist to talk to us and prescribe medication that would help us cope. The drugs did help some until the next day when I stood there over my mother's open casket trying to say goodbye. My heart couldn't handle it. They had to carry me to the car. I wasn't able to accept that she was dead and begin to say goodbye until they started to lower the casket in the ground.

Grandma Lupita and most of the family members

that attended remained behind, but I could not. I wanted to get out of there. Driving back to the hotel, Ms. Doyle made it clear that I was welcome to live with her if I wanted.

"Am I welcome too?" Sam asked. "I don't have a house anymore."

"That's just the drugs talking," Ms. Doyle answered. "And you're upset right now but soon you will forgive your father."

"It's not the drugs talking," Sam said. "That man took our mothers away from us. I don't ever want to see his face again."

I agreed. I didn't either.

"Well, I would love to have you until you're ready to return home," Ms. Doyle answered.

Afraid for Sam's life, we decided to leave DR, where the killers probably still were. We drove straight to the hotel, grabbed Sam's green duffel bag and the rest of our stuff, and headed to the airport. We took the first flight to the U.S., not caring it was going to Miami. Sam said it would be better, because she was sure there would be tons of reporters at the airport waiting for flights from DR. We took another flight into LaGuardia Airport, figuring Kennedy would be the expected airport. It worked. We were not harassed at the arrival gate, where Giovanni and Molly were waiting for us.

Sam demanded we take her straight to her house. She seemed possessed, so much so, that when Giovanni hugged and kissed her she never hugged him back or even once looked at him.

"The FBI is at your house, Sam," Giovanni said as he pulled our luggage from baggage claim. "They demanded that I call you, but you never answered. Probably because you were in flight."

"They searched your house from top to bottom, Sam," Molly said. "What are they looking for?"

"I know exactly what they are looking for," Sam answered and said nothing else.

"Is it true Sam?" Giovanni asked. "Did your father cause those people to die?"

Sam refused to answer. We drove both Mr. Raider's car and Sam's car to the front of Ms. Doyle's house. Sam hopped out of her car and opened the trunk. She grabbed her duffel bag, unzipped it, and dumped its contents into the trunk, walking back to her father's car with the empty bag.

"I need your help, guys," she said. "There is something I need to retrieve from the house."

We all agreed, except for Ms. Doyle, who stayed behind on the second floor of her house. She used her binoculars to lookout for us in case the FBI, who were still sitting in front of the house, decided to come inside when we were there.

All four of us made our way over the fence into Justin's backyard, over the fence between his house and Sam's, then to her back door. Carrying her empty bag, Sam led us directly into the panic room. She locked the door as we all went inside. She pressed on both sides of the wall beside the monitors until a panel slid to reveal a large safe the size of a double-door fridge. Sam put the code in and opened the door.

"This is the blood money the FBI is looking for. I'm taking all of it," Sam said. "Help me haul it out of here."

Sam believed there was over forty million dollars in the safe. Not that we didn't want to help, but we were concerned about getting arrested. Sam convinced us by explaining the plan she had devised, but we were stunned by the quick and strange way Samantha's mind worked.

Two large duffel bags already held most of the money. We piled as much as we could in Sam's green one. When it was full, Sam grabbed a roll of garbage bags from the kitchen. We double-bagged and filled the plastic ones until there was nothing left in the secret compartment. Giovanni carried the garbage bags on the back of his neck one at a time, because that was the only way he could manage them.

Sam, Molly and I had to work together to half-carry, half-drag the garbage bags. It took a number of trips, but we got the bags to the first fence, where Giovanni and Sam "1, 2, 3" heaved them over. This process was repeated at the other fences until we finally made it to Ms. Doyle's house. While we took the bags the last leg of the journey, Sam ran back to pack some keepsakes in a little backpack, including some pictures of her mother. Sam turned back for her last look at the house of lies and discovered she wasn't satisfied.

"I can't believe we're done!" I said trying to get her attention.

"Almost," Sam said.

"What now?!" said Giovanni.

"You all stay here. Ophelia, come with me." The look on her face made me worry she wasn't in her right mind, but Samantha had kept faith. She was still my big sister. Even though the wedding never took place, here we were together, as a team. I could not say no.

When Sam grabbed a full one-gallon gas can from her garage, I got an inkling of what she had on her mind. With all the anger I had in my heart, I thought it would feel redeeming.

"I'm gonna burn that effing place to the ground," she whispered in a cold voice.

We took out another gas can–this was the big five-gallon kind, which was more than half full. Back in the house, we resolved to start with the panic room.

We started fires in the room and surrounding halls. Sam chose the panic room because she wanted the center of the fire to be raging beyond control before the FBI agents outside detected it. As we doused the rooms with gasoline, I felt like the hand of justice.

"This house was bought with dirty money," Sam said. "I'm making sure he has nothing to come home to."

I got chills when she said that, and I'm embarrassed to admit how good she sounded. We walked around the bedrooms pouring gasoline all over the wooden floors and beds and into the closets full of clothing. I remember being amazed at how much gas could fit in one of those containers. With the last bit, we created a line downstairs to the kitchen like we had seen on TV. Sam walked up to the stove, grabbed a napkin from the counter and lit it.

"Come on, Sis!" she said. We walked backwards out of the kitchen. Sam dropped the napkin at the back door and we took off running. We jumped the fence and looked at each other, struggling to catch our breaths. We looked back through the wood panels to watch the kitchen become engulfed in flames.

When we arrived back at Ms. Doyle's house, and she smelled the gas on us, she froze.

"Oh my Lord," she yelled. "Have you lost your mind?!"

Ms. Doyle rushed up to her favorite spying window, and we followed.

"Pray to God you don't hurt anybody," she yelled.

We could see the flames going in the house through the upstairs window. Sam and I looked at each other and grinned with satisfaction. We sat down trembling on the bed. As the windows broke and the fire accelerated, though, our feelings began to change. Our trembling turned to shaking, and we began to cry in unison. Overwhelmed by the events of the past three days and what she had done, Sam grabbed her head in both hands and began to scream. I fell over and sobbed. Giovanni tried to comfort Sam, but she pushed him away.

Sam rolled over and wrapped her arms around me.

"You're my family, now." We sobbed together.

Giovanni looked helplessly at Ms. Doyle and Molly, who were staring at the fire in disbelief. It wasn't long before we heard sirens from the fire trucks.

Eventually, Sam wiped her tears, walked over to Giovanni and apologized to him. We all stood together watching the house, now completely ablaze, and the firefighters arranging their hoses for battle the fire. In a half hour, when it seemed clear the neighboring houses were safe, we were all relieved.

After a long silence, Ms. Doyle was the first one to speak. "One time, I tried to run my boyfriend over with a car."

Molly chimed in, "We should burn Justin's house next."

It was wrong, but we laughed anyway. There was nothing else to do but laugh and cry.

12

THE RESIDUAL EFFECT

For the next five days, Giovanni called Sam, but she never answered. She never showed up at Juilliard. Ms. Doyle begged her to go, but Sam refused and told her she didn't want to dance anymore. She never got out of bed during the daytime and hardly ate. All she did was lie in bed and watch the news, needing to understand what was happening. Every half hour, the story of her father and the suspicious burning of the house in Greenwich showed on the news.

Sam felt like her horror story with the detail constantly being reported around the world. And she was right. Sam watched closely as people from Darfur weighed in on the DR killings and the beheading of two more people Sam didn't know in New York City by the Genocide Retribution Army of Darfur. G.R.A.D. had become a force to reckon with in Darfur and across Africa and this only increased their popularity.

The media assumed that G.R.A.D. burned the Raider home, and perhaps the FBI had as well, because they never came around to question us. Anyone who was accused of helping to fuel genocide across Africa, as well as their property, had become a target, whether the accusations were clearly based in fact or not. The spirit of revenge was out of control. The devil walked the entire earth.

After a couple of weeks, Sam tried to return to some sense of normalcy, but she was no longer the same young girl we knew. She still had not returned to school, but she agreed to see Giovanni when he traveled out to Ms. Doyle's and demanded to see her.

The conversation was disjointed and argumentative.

"You're so talented, Sam," Giovanni finally said, trying not to react to her verbal barbs. "You have the opportunity to become one the best dancers in the world. This is not the time to give up on your career."

"I'm sure there were a lot of little children murdered who had dreams of becoming someone great, but they will never see that day, will they?" Sam ranted. "I'm sorry. You can stay cocooned in your own little world, but I can't. You have no idea what's going on, do you? I'll figure out what I'm supposed to do, but I'm not going back to school. Get it?" She barked as she turned and walked away.

Giovanni followed. "You think you're the only one who wants to right the wrongs of this world," Giovanni yelled behind her. "But we are not God. We just have to try to be good."

Sam turned around and pushed him hard on the chest. "It wasn't your father who was responsible for the deaths of thousands of people," Sam screamed. "You don't have to live with that, do you? Do you?!"

"I know you're hurting, but don't push me away!" Giovanni said. "I want to be with you. I want to help. Let me help you."

Samantha looked in his eyes and saw how sincere he looked. Suddenly, her face softened. She closed the distance between them, put her hands around his waist, and started to cry on his chest.

"I'm so angry, and I can't help it," Sam muttered. "I'm so sad inside."

Sam dried her tears with her shirt and looked up at Giovanni. Maybe if you were more concerned about the things that are happening in the world you could help me. If you don't feel the same sense of responsibility as me, I think you better leave."

It was obvious that Sam felt closed off. Everything she had believed was true had been blown to shambles. She walked away from Giovanni, headed to her bedroom, and slammed the door. Sam stared at in the mirror, barely recognizing herself.

That day, when I arrived home from my first day back from school, I found Ms. Doyle talking to Sam. "Sometimes we are forced to do the right thing," she said. "Unfortunately, it might come at some expense."

"What are you planning on doing, Sam?" I asked. "Why is Ms. Doyle saying that?'"

"I have decided to go to Darfur and distribute the blood money."

I began to panic. "If those GRAD thugs find out who you are, you'll be dead," I warned. "I can't lose you too!"

"I know, but it's the risk I have to take. Sometimes, the sins of the father fall on his children," Sam replied. "I can't live with myself if I don't do this."

"Ms. Doyle, tell her not to go," I begged. "Please!"

"I absolutely will not," Ms. Doyle answered. "She's grown up enough to make her own decisions."

I became angry and walked out into the greenhouse. I became startled when a male voice came from behind one of the plants.

"Very calming, isn't it?" He said. "Don't be scared." The man resembled the one who had killed my mother. "I'm Nuango, and you must be Ophelia," he said as he made his way towards me.

Terrified, I ran back into the house and slammed the door behind me.

"There is a man out there," I said breathlessly to Sam and Ms. Doyle.

"Calm down, Ophelia," Sam said. "He was sent by the Embassy of Darfur in response to my inquiries. We invited him here."

Ms. Doyle opened the back door and started to laugh with the man.

"I am sorry I scared you, Ophelia," he said. He came and shook my hand. When he told me I was very pretty, I was charmed. We went into the living room, where he sat in a chair, and I shared a couch with Sam and Ms. Doyle.

Nuango turned out to be a thirty-six-year-old diplomat who had survived the genocide but lost both parents. He was taken in by a nonprofit organization that contacted his sister in England. He was given a refugee visa and sent to live with her. He made good on the opportunity by earning a scholarship to the prestigious Oxford University in England after two years of high school. While at Oxford, he studied business law and world politics, graduating near the top of his class. Against the wishes of his sister, he returned home to Darfur to help the government rebuild. Eventually, he was sent to the embassy in New York to work with other governments and nongovernmental agencies to rebuild Darfur.

He exuded confidence, intelligence, and a sense of calmness that was uncanny. Combined with his muscular physique and facial features chiseled from stone, it was hard not to stare at him. He was unassuming, yet he demanded everyone's attention just by his presence. Ms. Doyle was completely overtaken by his aura and sat with her hands at her jaw. She stared at him like a piece of cake just out of reach. While Sam inquired about banking laws and procedures, Ms. Doyle kept interrupting by asking personal questions and being inappropriate.

"Do you know how handsome you are?" she asked. "Would you date a cute white woman like myself?"

The only thing that distracted any of us from Nuango was a phone call that Sam received from a lady who had bought a couch from our yard sale. While Sam talked on the phone, Nuango continued to talk to Ms. Doyle, answering some of her questions in a playful manner.

"I have to go," Sam said after she hung up the phone. "A woman from the nursing home found a letter from my mother tucked in the side of the couch. She understood the importance of the letter after hearing our story on the news."

Samantha had donated her car, considering it another blood trophy. Ms. Doyle's car had recently been brought back into working order, so Sam had been able to use it instead. Sam and I climbed into the convertible Jaguar and sped to the assisted living facility in Mount Vernon. We walked intently to the receptionist, where Sam pointed out the couch to me. The receptionist directed us to the door of the lady, who invited us in.

The woman introduced herself as Justine. "That chair in the lobby has been a blessing. Every little bit of elegance means a lot at this age." Justine explained that she had dropped one of her pills and found a letter between the cushions. We shared amazement that the letter had not been lost when the chair was moved. "The letter's been sitting on my kitchen counter for weeks. When I saw you on the news, I asked the woman who works here who got the chair from you."

Justine, in her frailty, walked slowly into the kitchen and retrieved the letter. She handed it to Sam, who read eagerly to herself.

My dear Samantha,

I write this letter with a heavy heart. I have found out that the man I have loved and trusted to care for me has now put my life and yours into great jeopardy. Your father has done terrible things, and there are brutal men who want revenge and others who want to keep this all a secret who could be just as dangerous. I know it is hard to believe your father could act so wrongly, but you must believe me.

I have tried to leave, but your father he has control of all of the money, and I don't know how I can support you. So I am going to make arrangements as soon as I can to send you to your Aunt Carol.

I have a list of accounts and the names of the men your father committed these crimes with. It is in a safety deposit box at Chase Bank in midtown. The key and box number are hidden in the basket of your bicycle.

If my fears are realized and I am harmed, please do not return to your father. He is not what he seems. I am so sorry I trusted this man. I am scared, but more scared for you than for myself, because you are the most important thing in the world to me. I love you, my dear.

Sam could barely stand after she read the note. Justine sat Sam down and embraced her, while I read the letter.

When I was done, Justine told us she had read the letter. "I hope that is alright. I can imagine how heavy your heart must be, Samantha, but you cannot let anger and fear take you over. You must try to look at this as a new beginning. Put your life in God's hands and he will protect you in this life or in the hereafter."

We listened to Justine, who spoke slowly and calmly. Sam nodded at her through her tears. She began to feel, once again, that she was being blessed by the things she relinquished at the yard sale.

"If you are able to get that information, be sure to use it well," Justine continued. "The important thing in life is not what you know, but what you do with your knowledge."

I told Justine what Sam was thinking of doing, hoping she would give Sam different advice than Ms. Doyle had. Justine listened carefully, then looked down while she thought about what to say.

"I think that sooner or later we all have to stop living for ourselves and live for others. Whether it's a big thing like what you're thinking of doing, Sam, or something smaller, we have to try. I understand your fear, Ophelia, but if Sam does the right thing, God will protect her. This life is only a doorway. The house is beyond."

I was hardly reassured, but I realized there was nothing I could do to change Sam's mind. She was resolved as she drove us home. She knew what she had to do. Sam asked me to go into her backpack and pull out the book in which she had kept all of her contacts from the yard sales. When we were parked in Ms. Doyle's garage, she searched through the book and found the contact information of the pastor who had taken the bike. On the phone, he told her that the bike had arrived safely in the Philippines. It was being enjoyed, as he had promised, by a little girl named Lele. He did not have a way, though, to reach her by phone.

"I guess I'll have to fly to the Philippines to find Bugsy," she said.

"You named your bicycle Bugsy? I guess you were weird even before all this happened."

Sam sounded like a child again as she told me how she used to ride Bugsy to the seashore when her father thought she was practicing violin.

"I've never even ridden a bike before," I said to Sam, thinking how there was so much more to life than I knew.

"I would love to teach you that too," Sam said. "But, I'm sorry I have to leave."

Rather than going inside, Sam reopened the garage door and turned the key in the ignition. Sam drove to the local bike store and bought me a Schwinn almost exactly like Bugsy. We drove to a big parking lot and stayed there until the skies grew dark, Sam running behind the bike and holding the seat to help me balance. I figured it out on my own the second time she let go, but that was only after I crashed into a garbage can, scratching up my knees and elbows on the rough asphalt. Sam ran over to me and sat beside me, kissing my elbows and knees sweetly. I used the opportunity as one last ditch effort to dissuade Sam from leaving.

"Sam, don't you wanna dance anymore? Don't you want to have a normal life?"

"I don't even know what normal is anymore." Sam said. "Do you?"

"No, but I want to live, and I'm not talking about the hereafter. I want to grow up and see what my future holds. I've had enough danger in my life.

"Well, that's what you should do then, Ophelia. But I feel like I've been living in a box all my life, and now I just want to see what's outside that box."

It was an answer that would fundamentally change the way I looked at Sam's decision. It wasn't only about revenge, or solving the puzzle of her Mamma's death, or even something abstract like Justice, though I admired her righteousness. When she used the phrase "living in a box," I got it, because it reminded me of the little apartment in the Bronx that I wasn't allowed to leave without my Mamma. For years, I yearned to see more of what was outside that little box. It wasn't until my mother took me to DR for the first time that I felt free. Playing the violin for the first time also made me feel that way. But now the violin had negative associations for me as well.

I needed to occupy my time and make myself happy if Sam wasn't going to be around. "Will you help me find a piano teacher," I asked?

13

THE GOOD SAMARITAN

Sam arrived in the Philippines two days later. It was obvious the note had profoundly affected her. Her mother had called her from the grave to wage a crusade against the people who truly caused the death of our mothers. Sam had made further arrangements with the pastor of Full Gospel Mission, who had contacts there. First, though, she wanted to see something she had discovered in her online research of the Philippines.

As soon as she came off the plane, she exchanged one hundred thousand dollars for pesos and hired a cab to take her to the city dump. Armed with a video camera, laptop, and enough funds to help whoever she wished, she went to capital city to see the garbage pickers at the dump she had read about. Just as advertised, there she found hundreds of young orphans and runaways living there, rummaging through arriving truckloads of garbage for something to sell for pennies.

Her taxi driver, Manuel, insisted on accompanying Sam into the dump. He kept Sam from being mobbed as she distributed a thousand pesos to every orphan she saw. Sam realized the wisdom of having a local with her and hired Manuel for the week for ten thousand pesos, more money than he had ever seen at one time. Manuel became an invaluable assistant. He translated for her to the children–a bus would arrive the next day at noon. Any child who chose to get on board the bus as long as there was room would be given free passage to the Panay

Islands and given shelter in an orphanage. While the orphanage sponsored by the Full Gospel Mission was mostly full, the pastor had helped her locate a newly established mission that could take the children.

Most of the children, knowing that strangers preyed on young people in the slums, were unwilling to trust this total stranger with piles of money and a story too good to be true. Some, though, were hungry enough to take the risk and agreed to be ready to go.

Sam had extended her cell phone plan, so she was able to call us that night. She sounded exhausted but very happy about what she had already been able to do. Molly told her she wasn't the only one who had gotten lucky. Although Nuango was much younger than Ms. Doyle, he had agreed to go with her on her first date in twelve years! After the date, they arrived back home by taxi, stumbling through the door, tumbling over the furniture like wild animals. Soon they were in her bedroom, and I had decided it was a good time to put in earbuds and listen to music.

Sam had suggested getting a recommendation for a piano teacher from my music teacher. Ms. Scholman had highly recommended a sixteen-year-old boy, to our surprise. He was the classically-trained son of an Israeli mother and an American Jew from Brooklyn. He was a child prodigy who had played Carnegie Hall for the mayoral inauguration party when he was ten years old. Shiloh Sheinbaum's performing career had not become lucrative, but he was making good money doing lessons. He charged an exorbitant fee but a price that Ms. Doyle thought was worthwhile since he would understand what it was like for me to have such gifts as a youth. I told Sam about my first lesson–which was awesome!–and she teased me about Shiloh, asking me if he was cute. He was.

Sam promised to send me some .mp4s that she had taken at the dump. After she chatted a little with Ms. Doyle, she hung up and sent the videos. When they finally came through, we were dumbfounded. Young children, some of them naked, eating garbage and drinking dirty water. I prayed that night for those children and started to feel really good about what Samantha was trying to do. Before I went to bed, I put on big headphones and practiced on a new, full-sized Yamaha keyboard. I thought about the contrast between my comfortable life and their bare existence and tried to channel the emotion into my playing.

The word had spread about Sam's offer, so even though most kids weren't willing to go when she made it initially, the bus was still filled to capacity before it left at 12:30 p.m. Some of the kids had to share beds at first at the orphanage, but with an infusion of funds from Sam, the facility began expanding immediately.

Sam chartered a boat back to the mainland, where she was picked up by Manuel. He took her to the Full Gospel Mission orphanage, where she inquired about Lele and Bugsy. It wasn't long before Lele came riding up to Sam and Manuel on Bugsy.

"There you are, my old friend!" Sam exclaimed. "I see you have taken good care of my friend, Lele."

"Are you here to take it back, Miss Raider," Lele asked.

"Absolutely not," she smiled. "And please call me Sam. But I do want to take it for a ride, if you don't mind." Sam did not want to explain about the key, so she decided to wait for a chance to search the basket when Lele wasn't watching.

"Sure, if you take me with you," Lele answered.

Lele let Sam take her place on the seat and climbed onto the axle of the back wheel. She held on to Sam's shoulders and they rode down the hill and into a green little valley that stood at the bottom of the hill. Reluctant to turn back, Sam soon reached the town of Guimaras, the site of a monastery. After seeing three of the men walking outside the green building in the garden, Sam stopped the bike and asked Lele about them. The Trappist order of Catholic monks there also offered a sanctuary for others who wanted to draw closer to Christ. Sam got off the bike and walked towards the gate. One of the monks walked up to the gate and opened it.

"Welcome sister," he said while smiling at her.

The word "enlightenment" took hold of Sam's mind as she walked through the gate. Sam had read about monks in other countries and was always intrigued by men and women who choose to live such simple lives. Now, more than ever, she was able to recognize the wisdom in their way of life. In response to Sam's questions, the monk explained that he had taken a vow in order to seek a closer union with God. They sought salvation and sanctification by adhering to Christ's teaching.

"To free ourselves from the cares of this world," he said, "we dedicate ourselves fully to prayer and holy reading, study, and meditation."

Sam was fascinated by the monks. She learned that they offered a retreat where three Americans were staying for two weeks. Sam asked and was granted the permission to return the next day early in the morning to meditate with the monks.

Sam and Lele took turns riding the bike back to the orphanage, sometimes walking it when the way was too steep. Manuel was sitting in the car when they returned. When he and Lele went inside to get something to drink, Samantha saw her opportunity to retrieve the key and safety deposit box number that her mom had told her about. She lifted the lid to the basket and felt around inside. After she emptied the basket of Lele's doll and other small possessions, she could feel the key. She pulled up the lining inside the basket and took in her hand the key and the code, which was engraved on a rectangular piece of metal. Quickly, she tucked the lining back into place as best as she could and returned the doll and its friends to their little basket house.

She had it! Part of her wanted to have Manuel take her back to the airport immediately, but something told her to wait. Sam was supposed to leave in five days, but after three days with the monks, she decided to stay another week. Sam divided her time between mediation, study with the monks and making improvements at the orphanage. With the blessing of the pastor, Sam sent Manuel to organize a work team. They brought heavy equipment in order to transform the mountainside into a four-acre farm.

They turned the soil to prepare it for crops, built a large chicken coop, and fenced off areas for livestock. She had workman come from the city to install a satellite dish and computer classroom for the orphanage, which would also allow for communication with the rest of the world. By the time Sam left the Philippines, the orphanage was well on its way to becoming financially self-sustainable. Sam relished watching her ideas become reality.

Although Sam knew the Trappist lifestyle wasn't right for her, their practice of meditation and teaching helped her to work through the hate and anger she still felt since that terrible day when Gina was murdered and she learned the truth about her father. She couldn't leave it all behind in two weeks, but she learned some strategies for dealing with it when it threatened to overcome her.

After two weeks, her eagerness to open that safety deposit box returned. She expressed her gratitude to the monks with a donation, thanking them sincerely for their hospitality. Lele and the other children were very sad to see Sam go, and Samantha allowed herself to cry as well. She promised them, though, that they could video-chat with her every so often from their new computer classroom. Manuel took her back to the airport, where he refused to take further payment. He presented to her a basket of fruit and flowers that had been put together by the men and women who had been hired at the orphanage.

On the plane ride back Sam realized her passion and decided the key to her happiness depended on her philanthropic work.

Back in Manhattan, the safety deposit box opened to reveal an expanding file folder full of photocopies. Invoices, wire transfer receipts, and email transcriptions documented the involvement of bankers and government officials on three continents. Sam arrived back at Ms. Doyle's unsure what her next step should be.

"You need to give this to the FBI, Sam," Ms. Doyle urged.

"You want me to give this to the same government that allowed this to happen for twenty years? The FBI must have known about this, because they knew about Dad. And still they let us go to that wedding where Gina's family was slaughtered."

"As impressive as you are, Samantha, don't you think this is a bit much for a teenager to take care of?" Ms. Doyle asked. "Maybe this folder is what the FBI needed to put your father and his accomplices in jail."

Their disagreement went on for a while in this fashion until they agreed to ask Nuango for advice. When they had arrived at that satisfactory plan, I ran over to the piano and began to play. Sam joined me and played something to accompany me at the higher end of the keyboard. Amazed that she could play the piano just as well as the violin, I ran upstairs and grabbed the violin. We found some sheet music we were both familiar with and played together for about an hour.

We were interrupted by Ms. Doyle, who told us that someone was outside the gate. Sam looked at the camera on the intercom and saw it was her father sitting in the back of a taxi. Dismayed, Sam turned and walked away from the camera.

"What do you want me to do, Sam?" Ms. Doyle said. "We can't just leave him sitting there. Do you want me to tell him you're not here?"

"Tell him nothing," Sam yelled. "Don't say a word. I owe him nothing."

The very thought of her father infuriated Samantha. It took all her mental strength to stay inside and not go outside, drag him out the car and beat him to a pulp.

Her father's voice came over the intercom. "Sam, I have paid dearly for what I did," he said. "Please talk to me." When Sam didn't respond, he raised his voice. "I will kill myself if you won't talk to me!"

Now I was just as angry as Sam. How dare he, after what he had done, try to manipulate Sam in that way! Sam had successfully contained her anger, but when I recalled my mother's murder that started to play in my head like a movie, I lost control. I opened the front door, dashed through the gate to the taxi, and started jabbing him in the face with my violin bow. I scratched him up pretty well before the taxi driver could grab me.

Sam and Ms. Doyle came running outside.

"You're not my father anymore!" Sam yelled. "You are a parasite, and I want you out of my life! Never contact me again!"

Sam demanded for the taxi driver to let me go. As soon as he did, I got in one more jab before Sam grabbed my arm.

"He's not worth it," she said.

We all turned and went back through the gate, which Ms. Doyle closed behind us.

"I'm still your father!" Mr. Raider yelled as we walked away.

It took a lot for us to calm down. Luckily, Nuango arrived minutes after, and helped to calm us down. His charm was undeniable.

He got the idea of watching the altercation on the security video.

After we watched for a while, Ms. Doyle spoke up.

"You ever thought about fencing, Ophelia?" Ms. Doyle asked.

"Fencing? Never." I answered.

"You should. You have a wicked thrust."

We all laughed while Nuango rewound the videotape.

"No, I'm thinking track and field," he said, after pressing play. I watched myself running through the gate holding my bow almost like a javelin.

Sam and I laughed hysterically at the two angry girls on the video who now seemed like two complete strangers. We were in good spirits again.

Ms. Doyle disappeared and returned with three sweaters and a sports jacket she had made.

"This is a good time to share this with you," she said. "I have started to design clothes again, this time for men. Nuango has been my muse. I can't stop thinking of things that will look good on that amazing body of yours."

Nuango unleashed a big kiss on her lips then took the clothing.

"I'm going to model these for you, my love," he said. "Be right back."

"Mmmm. Now I know why my ex-husband was so eager to rob the cradle," Ms. Doyle said.

After we had good laugh, Sam asked why Ms. Doyle had kept the fact that she was designing again a secret.

"I had to see if I was still any good at it first. I can't tell you what it's like to discover yourself all over again. That boy has brought back my passion for everything I enjoyed doing."

"Everything?" Sam teased.

"Everything!" Roared Ms. Doyle, setting off another round of laughter.

Nuango came out in one of the sweaters and the jacket. He strutted back and forth across the living room as we clapped, cheered, and cat called.

"These are so unique," Nuango said. "The colors in this sweater are perfect for me. Thank you, Vanna."

Ms. Doyle blew him a kiss, then begged him to try the other sweaters on. Sam and I were delighted to be there at the rebirth of the Vanna Doyle Collection as an innovating force in men's fashion.

14

RIGHTING THE WRONGS

Late that night, Sam had a long talk with Nuango about the landscape of politics in Africa after the genocide began. Not being sure who to trust, Sam began to regard the folder of documents that her mother left for her as a weapon. She hoped Nuango's insights would help her determine how to wield that weapon. Sam never told Nuango what she had, but she did tell him she had a significant sum of money that she wanted to go back to the people of Darfur.

Nuango explained that in many areas affected by her father's criminal banking syndicate, and particularly in Darfur, many factions continued to jockey for power.

The severity of Darfur's endemic corruption meant no organization could be entirely trusted to put the needs of the people ahead of their own desire for power and wealth. As a result, the U.N. workers, nongovernmental agency employers, and religious and humanitarian volunteers could not deliver food and medicine to the hundreds of thousands of people suffering there without putting themselves in danger also.

Sam had many questions about G.R.A.D and its relationship to the corrupt politicians and various factions. Nuango explained that the group was a well-organized, secret organization of Darfur rebels that was made up of educated men and defected soldiers from Darfur. G.R.A.D. wanted to overthrow the government, but this put them in conflict with other militia groups that the government had made agreements with and empowered to kill citizens. Sam was shocked to learn that for all purposes, the genocide was ongoing. Over two million people had been displaced since it began. The Sudanese Air Force was still actively bombing civilians and citizens were still being attacked on the ground by the Sudan Army and associated Janjaweed.

Sam listened to Nuango and asked questions for more than two hours. She began to understand that distributing money in Darfur would be even more difficult than she had imagined. Overwhelmed by what she had heard, Sam went to her bedroom to think about what she had learned. It weighed on her for the next two days as she considered what course of action to take. Sam spent hours reading online about Darfur.

After a week, she had made a decision even more shocking than the decision to burn down her own home. She called Ms. Doyle, Molly, Giovanni, and me into the living room and steeled herself to share her plan. She was nervous, because she knew she was risking her relationship with the people who now meant the most to her. The woman who believed in her most. The girl who had trusted her to help her manage a pregnancy. The first boy she ever loved. Her new sister.

She thought about what Justine, the wise woman in the nursing home, had said to her. The important thing in life is not what you know, but what you do with your knowledge.

The documents she had in her possession were incriminating, to be sure, but nothing ensured that the evidence would make a real difference. She had to use her weapon in the most effective way possible.

Sam summarized for us the chaotic situation in Sudan and why she didn't think giving the documents to the F.B.I. or the U.N. would make any real difference. Corruption was two widespread and any honest workers seemed to have their hands tied. Doing what she could to stop the ongoing genocide, she argued, was more important than the indictment of a few bankers, who could use their resources to drag out the court cases indefinitely. She only knew of one rebel group who, while capable of real brutality–perhaps even fanaticism–had not shown themselves to be motivated by greed.

"Soon, I will be leaving for a refugee camp in Chad. I'm going to take the folder to the leaders of G.R.A.D.," she finally announced, "the only people who are in a real position to use the information as a weapon against genocide and corruption."

We could not believe our ears. Instead of turning the files over to the authorities, she was going to give them to the people who murdered Gina and her brothers and maimed Mr. Raider.

"So you're going to befriend the man who killed my mother," I said.

"I never said he was going to be my friend."

"But you are going to reward him for what he did?"

"I loved Gina too, and I am furious about what he did to you, but this is bigger than just us, Ophelia. The real enemies are the people like my Dad who steal other people's resources and the thugs who run the Sudanese government who wage war against their own people. They are my enemy. And G.R.A.D. is the enemy of my enemy. Only in that sense can I consider that man a friend. I know you feel like I am betraying Gina and I hate that my choice is painful to you, but I don't see how the genocide can stop unless men responsible are held responsible.

"What about Mamma?!" I screamed. "Was she responsible?"

"Of course not, but thousands of people are dying. Gina was an innocent victim, also, but that doesn't mean that we don't do what we can to put an end to this! No one but G.R.A.D. can cut off the money that is funding the Sudanese government's war on its own people."

"This is insane," I said. If you do this, you are no longer my sister!" I stormed to my bedroom.

Sam watched me leave the room and then dropped her head in grief. Then she got angry and yelled after me. "Don't forget that he killed my mother too! I'm sacrificing too!"

After a pause, Ms. Doyle tried a different tack. "How do you know they won't just kill you?"

"I don't." Sam answered.

"Samantha, there is sometimes a very thin line between brave sacrifice and arrogant foolishness. In this case, the line is very thick. This is a big mistake!" Ms. Doyle said, but immediately regretted letting her anger get the best of her.

"I won't be going until I have hired a unit of bodyguards." I'm leaving day after tomorrow for Virginia to talk to Lyceum."

Giovanni spoke up. "Lyceum? You are hiring mercenaries?! Your own little army? You're a radical militant now? I don't want to be a part of this anymore, Sam. You've gone insane!"

"There's the door," Sam said, without as much as a pause. She had thought this through carefully over days. Her decision was made, and she knew it was probably going to cost her.

Giovanni grabbed his backpack and walked out the door. Molly turned to Sam and stared at her.

"Sam, you know how I have trusted your wisdom, and you know that I have looked up to you. But now it seems like you think you are God. Sure you're smart, but you're still just a teenager."

"I don't think I'm God. That's not fair. I'm doing what I think God wants me to do. There's a difference. I may be a teenager, but I've got a boatload of cash and some serious dirt on evil men. If I can possibly make a difference, and I don't try, what am I then?

"I don't know, but I'm pretty sure you aren't the messiah either," Molly retorted before she walked out the front door.

"Are you going to help me, Ms. Doyle?" asked Samantha.

"I don't feel good about this, Sam. I'm not going to say yes now, but if you get in trouble and need resources, or can find a way to help people without financing terrorism, I hope you will ask me for help then. I'll decide at that time what to do."

"Whatever God wants to happen, that's what's going to happen," Sam said.

"People have free will, Sam. Do you think God wanted the genocide to happen in the first place? That certainly happened." Ms. Doyle stood up to signal that she was done talking. Sam didn't push her to stay, but merely thanked her for listening and considering her request for support. Ms. Doyle accepted Sam's thanks with a hug, but Sam still read disappointment in the way her only remaining mother figure carried herself to her bedroom.

When Molly had walked out the door, Sam had assumed it was a sign of Molly giving up on her like I had. Molly was more worried than mad though. She had immediately walked over to Justin's house and started banging on the door with utter disregard for his parents. When Justin came to the door and saw Molly, he surprised her by calmly inviting her to come in.

"I don't want to come in," Molly said. "I just came to tell you that your friend Samantha is going into a war zone tomorrow. You should make things right with her before she leaves."

Molly started to walk away but Justin followed behind her. When she stopped and turned, he faced her on the sidewalk.

"I know everyone is mad at me," he said. "I don't know what to do anymore. I mean...I care...I don't want to feel this way anymore."

"It's always about how you feel isn't it," said Molly. "I can't see how you acted like you loved me one second and then tried to bully me into killing our baby the next. Anyway, this isn't about us. This is about Sam."

"What is she up to now?" said Justin. "I saw you guys carrying those bags from her house, then I watched her burn the house down. I filmed it with my phone. Sam is crazy!"

Molly looked at Justin and simultaneously they started to laugh. What else could they do? Sam was definitely off the deep end, but they both remained loyal to her. Which they both knew was probably nuts! They both felt a sense of relief at having their first moment of friendship since he had abandoned her at the doctor.

"I'm sorry Molly," said Justin. "Sam told me I am a better man than my actions show. I want to be that better man, but I just can't risk losing the support of my parents. They'll kick me out of the house."

Molly did not answer. She started to pray within herself that Sam would have the right words for him. They walked back over to Ms. Doyle's and Molly went in to get Sam. Sam didn't hesitate to hug him. She saw the stress on his face. She knew him being there meant he still cared about her. Justin held her and started to tear up.

"I know the pregnancy has been hard for you," said Sam as she placed her hand on his chest. "I can forgive your mistakes if you try to make it right. I have one thing to say–you will never know who you really are until you relinquish the material things that are keeping you from being that good person. Your moral integrity and courage are far more important than anything your father or anyone else can give you."

Justin looked at her and found himself speechless. He walked over to Molly and kissed her cheek before hurrying away. For the first time in weeks, Molly felt confident that Justin might do right by his child, no matter what happened between them as a couple.

Molly was a born peacemaker. When it came to the people around her, it made her feel panicky when the people she care about are at odds. Her next move was to walk to my room hoping for the same kind of success she had had with Justin.

"You have to make things right with Sam before she leaves," she said as she climbed into bed with me. "You don't have to pretend you like what she's doing, but at least make up with her and say goodbye before she leaves. She's crazy, but you know she means well."

I turned and hugged her and was deeply grateful she was there to hold. I was feeling numb and helpless. Not knowing the future. Not knowing what to wish for anymore. I thought about how my dreams and hopes had played out. I thought about Mamma. I thought about losing Sam. I started to cry. I considered what Molly had said but was still conflicted about how to feel about Sam. I could not forgive her and I could not stand to lose her. I oscillated between anger and sadness. Molly held me until we both fell asleep.

I never said goodbye to Sam the following morning when she came to my room.

"I hope you will forgive me, Ophelia," she said and closed the door behind her.

I felt the same as the night before, only worse. I reached over to the nightstand and took two of the pills from the bottle the psychiatrist prescribed. I lay there waiting for the drugs to take effect. Eventually, I felt well enough to get up and try to lose myself in music. I called to ask Shiloh Sheinbaum over and we played hooky together. He must have sensed that something was wrong, because instead of being all business like normal to compensate for being an unusually young teacher, he showed a different side of himself that day.

"Wanna go play music in the subway with me?" he asked.

"In the city?" I asked in amazement.

"Yes, it will be fun!" he replied. "It will give you some good practice too. We'll find a busy spot in Grand Central."

"Yes, why not." I said and grabbed my violin.

"You have to tell me what's bothering you though when we get on the train," he said and flashed me a knowing smile.

Shiloh must have used this spot before, because he didn't even check the subway maps and walked directly to a little alcove where there would be room for a little audience without blocking foot traffic. He took his keyboard, a stand, and a small amplifier out of his bag, placed the keyboard on a stand, and began to play. At first, I just listened. So many people were staring, I became a little nervous. Eventually, though, I took a deep breath and concentrated on the music.

Then, Shiloh began to sing. I had never heard him sing before. His voice echoed off the walls and hit me, his talent nearly knocked me over.

It was a song that I had heard my mother singing at home, John Legend's Ordinary People. I chose my spots and played along.

Chorus–

We are ordinary people

We don't know which way to go

'Cause we're ordinary people

Maybe we should take it slow

This time we'll take it slow

By the time we finished the first song, we had a small audience begging for more. The crowd grew as Shiloh bellowed his tunes, dragging me into his escapade with imposed solo spots he signaled with a point of his finger. I hit a few bum notes, but mostly I surprised myself by improvising pretty well. It's not at all like playing from sheet music, but I had done enough noodling around freely in my room to play the notes I heard in my head.

The applause and compliments kept coming, and so did the dollar bills in the case of my violin. We took all the cash and gave it to a homeless woman who listened to us the entire time we were there. We spent some time in the Museum of Modern Art and then continued walking north into Central Park. Finally, we took the subway to Brooklyn for dinner at Shiloh's house. It wasn't long after we walked into his home, with its spectacular view across the East River and into Manhattan, that I thought I detected a serious rift between Shiloh and his parents.

"You didn't go to school today!" His mother yelled as soon as we walked in. "The school called."

"I don't need school, Mom," he said. "I'm a musician and a private music teacher. That's my job."

"It doesn't matter if you're a musician, you still need an education," his father added.

The argument continued, making me feel very out of place. His mother finally looked over and introduced herself to me.

"Shiloh says you're very talented," Ms. Sheinbaum said. "Don't follow his example and skip school. Your education comes first."

Her words sounded like something my own mother would say.

"I won't ma'am," I answered, eager to make a good impression.

"I guess you can stay for dinner in that case," she said a sarcastic tone. Then she turned to Shiloh. "Not sure if we should feed you anymore, boy."

"I make more money than you do, Mom," Shiloh said and started to laugh. "I can feed myself."

It took me a while to realize that they weren't trashing each other. This was just how they related to each other. Almost everything seemed like one big disagreement unless they were addressing me.

"So where are your parents, Ophelia?"

"Well, I don't know where my father is and...." I said as Shiloh cut me off.

"She lives in Connecticut with Vanna Doyle, Mom," he said.

"Vanna Doyle? Vanna Doyle, the designer?" she asked in her harsh Brooklyn accent. "You live with Vanna Doyle?"

"Yep, I do," I answered proudly.

"I loved her stuff. I used to shop at her boutique all the time," Mrs. Sheinbaum said.

"What happened to her?" she continued after walking towards the dining table. They still sell her classic designs in high end stores like Bloomingdales, although she disappeared from the fashion scene."

"She's coming back," I answered, hoping to stay on the subject of Ms. Doyle so I didn't have to tell my story. "She just started to design again."

"Wow. I am so happy to hear that. No one can make a better dress that that lady."

"Well, just between you and me, I think she's going to focus on men's wear."

"Really?" Mrs. Sheinbaum was excited to have the inside scoop. "How interesting!"

I told the story of Mr. Doyle's affair with Ms. Doyle's protégé but quickly reverted the focus on her new found interests in philanthropy. When I had run out of things to say, Shiloh began to discuss his desire to study music in Vienna with a descendent of Mozart. They refused, on the basis that he needed to finish school, which soon led to a bigger argument than before. They sounded angry, but as soon as the subject changed, everything was fine.

After dinner, Shiloh escorted me back to Grand Central on the train and made sure I boarded the correct train to Greenwich. I knew which one it was, but I liked the attention. He hugged me tightly before I went through the door and stood there as the train pulled off. Our time spent together that day had drawn us closer.

Strangely, the moment he was out of sight, Sam popped into my mind. The nerve of her! After the wonderful day with Shiloh, though, I was feeling much more forgiving than before, and I realized I did actually want to see her again.

Sam drove her car from Connecticut to Virginia with just enough clothes to cover the money in one of the duffel bags full of cash. She checked into the hotel, put her hair up into a tight bun as she had learned to do for ballet, and put on a professional, thin pinstripe black and gray suit out of Ms. Doyle's collection. Sam had told her "family" that she was going to hire bodyguards from Blackrock, a private security firm. She was being cautious and wanted them to believe she was being as safe as possible.

The truth was, though, she didn't feel she could trust that security firm, since their biggest contract was with the federal government. They might turn her in or steal the documents and deliver them to the FBI. Instead, Sam had poured through news stories for names of veterans who seemed talented and trustworthy after she did background checks on them.

Sam had set up a meeting with them at a Norfolk hotel. She had lured them with the possibility of high-paying civilian jobs. All five men were there in suits, introducing themselves to each other when she arrived.

Sam's outfit did the trick, and the men thought she was much older than seventeen. The bait had worked, now it was time for the switch.

Sam placed a briefcase on the table and opened it up to reveal five contracts that she expected them to sign. She removed them to reveal two-hundred-fifty-thousand dollars in cash. She then explained her real plan in broad terms. These were dangerous jobs in Africa.

"Fifty thousand now and fifty thousand when the job is done. All expenses paid." Sam divulged.

Two year's salary in cash for three months work? Sam had done her homework well. These men were a good fit for each other and had been out of action for some time. They all signed the contracts without giving serious consideration to what they were getting themselves into.

The next day, Sam called Nuango and asked for his help arranging a flight carrying 30,000 pounds of food and supplies, the five recruits, and her. Three days later, disguising themselves as simple aid workers serving the Sudanese refugees, they boarded a United Nations cargo plane. It took them to a landing strip in Chad about an hour from the Darfur border. Sam used the twenty-hour flight to get to know the men who were now responsible for her life.

Four of the men had served in Afghanistan, but no one had faced more gun battles than Sergeant Sean Nevers, who would be in command. He was a twenty-two years old, of French and Irish stock who had chased Bin Laden around the border of Afghanistan and Pakistan for two years, facing frequent artillery shelling from the Taliban and Al Qaeda. Sean had earned his purple heart, by running into the midst of an assault on a downed transport helicopter and rescuing four of its occupants. He had been shot three times and still had bullet fragments in his right hip. Sam picked Sean to lead her team because she felt he wouldn't lose his head in a precarious situation. Furthermore, he seemed to know a lot about the atrocities in Darfur and to have a sincere interest in contributing to the effort to end the genocide.

The other four members of the team had both excellent combat training and more specialized skills. James Fink and Jamie Harris were Black communications specialists in Afghanistan. They had been responsible at various times for enabling the troops to keep in touch with command and for gathering intelligence. They were going to help her link up her team and monitor the communications of G.R.A.D. or any other potentially unfriendly force. Frank Lombard and Brian Barnes were Irish-American Navy Seals who were decorated snipers. They would be focused on protecting the entire team with their excellent marksmanship.

A twenty-one hour plane with refueling stops gave Sam enough time to get to know the men who would be responsible for her life. All the men seemed intrigued by this mysterious, beautiful, and adventurous young woman. She told them about her father's wrongs and how she had transformed into this person who planned to make it right. She had adjusted her story, though, to leave them with the impression she was in her mid-twenties.

By the time the flight arrived in Chad, all of the men were more invested in the mission and had developed respect for Sam based on more than the money in her briefcase. The plane arrived in Chad, on the other side of Darfur from Sudan. Nuango had arranged trucks to carry the goods, as well as an armored SUV for the team. Also, there to greet the team was Ofi, the recipient of Sam's grandmother's stew pot. Ofi had been traveling back and forth between the U.S. and Chad bringing much needed medication and food to people in need, including her mother, who had severe diabetes and hypertension. Over 200,000 Darfur refugees lived in Chad in camps with conditions unfit for humans. Ofi had gladly agreed to be Sam's guide and translator.

"Little white girl, you have a lot of heart to come down here," Ofi said as she greeted Sam.

"So all this giving started from your experience at the yard sale. You must have really been blessed from that day on." Ofi was still under the impression that Sam was there only to do humanitarian work.

"Well, I would say it's been a blessing and a curse, what has happened to me since then," Sam answered, as they walked across the runway to the awaiting SUV. Sam and Ofi sat in the back and Sam explained the events of the past six months while the trucks were being loaded with forklifts. Ofi remarked that these items could do a lot of good, but made it clear there were many pitfalls to distributing goods in Chad and Sudan.

"My main concern is the Janjaweed militias, who attack convoys like these to take the food and supplies back to their own villages," Ofi said. "You must be careful at all times in the camps. Even if you are just going to the bathroom, take one of your men with you. There's a lot of violence against women in these camps."

"I hear you loud and clear," Sam said to Ofi.

"So is there anyone in your mother's camp that is from the rebel forces or G.R.A.D that you know and trust?" Sam asked Ofi.

Ofi immediately smelled trouble. "Now that you have told me your story, I'm worried you might try to do something foolish," Ofi said. "Those men will chop you up and send you back home in your suitcase."

"No, I am not here for revenge." I admire what G.R.A.D. is doing.

"But you gone mad, girl," Ofi responded. "After what they did to your father and him bride, you admire them?"

"This is not personal. It is much bigger than my family. I don't like all of G.R.A.D.'s tactics, obviously, but at least their motives are clear. Someone has to cut the flow of money that funds the genocide. I wish I could bring Gina back but my father had it coming."

"If you told me you had lost your marbles before you came here, I would have told you to stay there and get some help, because there is no psychiatrists out here," Ofi joked. "I can't believe you burned your house down."

It was then Ofi realized how serious Sam was.

"I know one rebel soldier from the Blue Nile region, but we would have to travel there to find him, because the government been bombing that region a lot lately," Ofi added. "I understand that you're upset at your father, but this is serious business. This is not America. Think about the most unruly parts in New York City, then multiply that ten times. I come here because I have no choice. This is where I was born, and I owe it to my mother, but this has been hell on earth from 2003."

Sam thought about Ofi's words. She knew she had the resources to make a difference, but would she be able to get the briefcase and the goods where they needed to go? She looked out the window and started to watch the trucks being loaded. She thought about what she had accomplished back in the Philippines. *Maybe I should focus her efforts in a more stable country.* She shook off that thought. *I can't give up before I even start.*

Eight trucks carrying the goods and Sam's crew were escorted by a single armed vehicle in front carrying United Nations peacekeepers. They traveled a half hour away through the harsh terrain to the Azize Refugee Camp where Ofi's family and friends awaited. Over ten thousand men, women, and children lived in that one camp, depending on non-profit organizations to provide their every need. It was the beginning of October, the end of the rainy season, so inaccessible roads had made it yet more difficult to get supplies there. The situation was dire. When Sam's team arrived, thousands of people swarmed the trucks, waiting for the peacekeepers and Sam's little group to distribute whatever they had. Several times, they had to fire shots in the air to keep everyone in order.

Sam was overwhelmed looking out at the sea of hungry and thirsty faces. Sam and Ofi, along with her five men, pushed their way through the crowd towards Ofi's family area. They walked for ten minutes through a walkway littered with tents on both sides. It seemed that every other tent had someone sweeping the dirt floor inside–trying to make things better in one of the few ways they could.

"We may not have much, but we are still a proud people," Ofi said. "We are not savages but the government treat us that way all the time. Many here are engineers, school teachers, and business owners hoping to go back home and start over."

"Do you think that is possible?" Nevers asked.

"The International Criminal Court just issued a warrant for the president of Sudan," Ofi explained. "But I doubt they will go after him. And it seems like the warrant has actually made the president more popular with certain groups."

"So you can't build your home back in Darfur until the fighting stops. Is it possible to build somewhere else?" Sam asked Ofi.

"I suppose it would be possible to build here in Chad if you had enough money to buy land and build houses, but we have lost everything," Ofi answered.

Finally, Sam saw a more specific plan taking shape in her imagination.

"Tomorrow, let's check into that, okay?" Sam said as she handed four of the dozen children nut bars she brought for herself. "We can make a difference here."

Upon arrival at Ofi family's tent, Sam saw the pot sitting on top of a wood fire. As Ofi introduced her to them, she described the yard sale where she had met Sam and said that Sam was there trying to help. The pot, with its thick glaze of colorful flowers, represented a significant asset in the context of the camp. The fact that the pot came from a young woman who would travel all this way made the pot even more special.

"My mom use to say her stew always tasted great because the pot was beautiful, inside and out," Sam said.

Ofi translated for her family, who shook their heads in appreciation and smiled with Sam. One by one, Ofi's family members hugged Sam and her burly companions. The youngest member of the family, Ofi's two-year old niece, wouldn't let go of Sam. The little girl said something and the whole family laughed.

"She thinks you're Rapunzel," Ofi said, as she picked up the children's book she had brought for her months before.

Sam's long blonde hair and slim face was an easy comparison for a three year old. From then on, Ofi's entire family called Sam "Rapunzel." Sam and all her men ate with Ofi's family, who were relatively well supplied because of Ofi, and told them she had plans to help them and many others in the camp. They left the tent around ten that night for the UN post at the front of the camp, where they unloaded their gear and hoisted an additional tent for their temporary dwelling. Sam called Ms. Doyle as soon as they were settled in to let her know she was safe. I could hear Ms. Doyle answering questions about me as I listened carefully to every word she said. I didn't want to care about Sam, but I had no choice. Sam had earned a special place in my heart. Still, I refused when she asked to talk to me. I wasn't ready to let down my guard.

She needed to know how strongly I felt and how upset I was with her.

"Are you going to be able to do what you went there to do, Sam," Ms. Doyle asked.

"I have a lot of help here, and Nuango really paved the way," Sam said. "We can start shipping tons of food here. It won't stop the killing but it will help a lot of people. That's something."

"What about the other thing?" Ms. Doyle asked. Sam walked out of the tent for privacy and told Ms. Doyle about Ofi's contact with one of the rebel soldiers. Ms. Doyle once again begged Sam to turn over the papers to the UN or FBI. She refused.

"Why can't you be satisfied with all the work and money you will pour in?" Ms. Doyle asked. "You'll be a bigger asset to everyone there alive than dead."

"Because my mother gave me this mission," Sam said. "I have to bring justice for her and the thousands who have suffered.

Sam explained to Ms. Doyle that she wanted to buy a large piece of land in Chad under Ofi's name and build a self-sustainable complex. Ms. Doyle was suddenly inspired to use her men's wear line to raise more funds so that she could be a bigger part of Sam's efforts. Maybe if she helped Sam's development efforts, she would eventually lose interest in G.R.A.D.

The next day, Ms. Doyle walked into the headquarters of a giant retail chain and sold her new, men's winter collection for millions. The executives could not believe their good fortune that they had bought exclusive rights to The Return of Doyle. While men's wear is not as lucrative as women's wear, just the added press that would come from this change would be extremely valuable. Within weeks, Ms. Doyle was on the cover of every fashion magazine. In all of them, she discussed the genocide in Darfur and gave a website address for donations.

Ms. Doyle's home became the head office for donations.

I became her unofficial personal assistant. We hosted a party almost every week and, knowing that what Sam was doing was far more difficult, we never felt burned out. Each week the party was more elaborate, attracting the rich and famous people from the entertainment and fashion world. Only when high-level banking executives started attending did these events feel awkward, but we resolved not to assume they were all the same as Mr. Raider.

I enjoyed every minute of it, especially when Ms. Doyle asked Shiloh and me to perform. This would pay off for Shiloh, as well, because at one of the parties, a prominent record producer was blown away by our performance and had his label offer Shiloh a record deal. Two weeks later Shiloh signed a record deal and started work on his first album. He called me his lucky charm and featured me on violin on several songs.

15

THE CONFLICTED

I had become involved in a fast-paced, high profile, and deeply fulfilling world. My work with Shiloh became a bigger part of my life than I expected because he began to count on me as a sounding board when making all kinds of decisions about his music, from music selections and arrangement, to the style of his playing and sound of the recordings.

Ms. Doyle also depended on me. As much as she loved her return to success, she also loved Nuango being in her life so she knew she had better not neglect him. After a few weeks of working nonstop, she put an away message on her phone directing people to me and escaped to Las Vegas with her man for some fun. They were in love, with a seemingly insatiable appetite for each other. When Sam called Ms. Doyle her first night from the border of Darfur, Ms. Doyle thanked her for causing her meeting with Nuango. Since then, he had helped Ms. Doyle set up an account so that Sam could access the donated money.

They planned to visit Chad to see the work Sam had done. Sam was eager to repay Ms. Doyle's and Nuango's support by impressing them with the good work they had helped make possible.

Sam and her entourage drove away from the refugee camp for about twenty minutes until they came to an area known for rich soil. Also, happily, there was running water and electricity nearby. They were searching for land to transform into the largest farm in the region. At a government office, they were informed of a two-hundred acre plot that they could purchase–it would support wells and running electricity and more importantly, growing plants.

A bright young government worker named Fawad told Sam and Ofi it would be much cheaper and easier if they formed a nonprofit organization before purchasing the land from the government. In that case, the land would be half the price and they could avoid most taxes. Fawad recommended a lawyer who could draw up a nonprofit charter for them very quickly and gave them a list of a few construction companies with good reputations.

After they spoke to the lawyer, he told them the charter for the Relinquish and Rise Organization would be ready the next day. They decided to choose Conway Construction, because they were the biggest company and had the political clout necessary to make it possible to expand their crew using engineers and laborers from the refugee camps.

The following day, Fawad and his lawyer friend came through with the papers and gave Sam the advantageous price for the land that he promised. Ofi, who was named as Chairperson of the new RRO nonprofit, signed the papers for the land.

Fawad gave them a survey of the land, which they immediately brought to the office of Conway Construction. Conway's in-office team assigned a foreman to return with Ofi to the camp for hiring and an architect and survey team to go with Sam to the property to make plans. Conway was taken aback by Sam's timetable, but when she offered to wire them two hundred thousand dollars as an advance to cover materials and overtime for their people, they agreed to expedite. The next day, Ofi and Sam sat with the foreman in the camp interviewing candidates. A handful of architects and engineers were hired to design more specific plans for each part of the project, as well as fifty laborers with various kinds of carpentry, plumbing, electrical, and agricultural experience. They also spread the word that these men and other men and women would be eligible to apply for permanent positions once the construction was near completion.

Needless to say, Ofi and Sam became camp rock-stars immediately. As news spread, not only refugees hoping for work started paying special attention to the visitors, but also the low-level informants for various rebel groups and government officials who hoped to get intelligence that they could trade for money or supplies.

Their notoriety was potentially very dangerous, but once the hiring was done, the Conway foreman took over the job of organizing the workers, so Sam and her team were able to get out of the camp. As Conway's advance team were moving heavy machinery towards RRO-one, the name Conway had assigned to the farm site, Sam's group was leaving the camp in search of Jon Bomi, Ofi's rebel contact, or any other lead that might get them in touch with G.R.A.D. Witnessing the progress that Sam had spearheaded in such a short time had quieted Ofi's objections. Sam had gone beyond just bringing supplies to keep people at the subsistence level. She was actually doing something that could make the area more self-sufficient. This young woman was a force to be reckoned with, and Ofi was going to do whatever she could to help her succeed.

As their armored SUV made its way east into Darfur, the team felt like they were going up the down escalator. Heading west was a stream of refugees carrying belongs into the relative safety of Chad. If they didn't already know they were going into hostile territory, it was clear now. About twenty-five slow miles past the Chad-Sudan border, they arrived at Geneina, the capital of West Darfur, where Ofi believed Bomi to be. Flat-topped, one- and two-story homes that were the same brown shade as the sand were offset by their blue shutters, as well as green trees sparsely dotting the landscape. They saw occasional billboards with smiling generals surrounded by propaganda in Arabic. Most alarming were the bullet holes they saw in every structure.

Following Ofi's direction, Lombard led up to what might have once been a school, but was now a barracks. The building was so shot up, Sam half expected it to collapse into dust before her eyes. Ofi got out of the SUV alone and walked slowly toward it. After only a few steps, Jon Bomi came out to greet her. He was a short, slim man with an AK-47 strapped onto his back. Somehow, Bomi's slight build made the weapon he was carrying even more menacing to Sam. Two more men followed him out of the building carrying rocket launchers and small firearms.

Sam's men kept their weapons concealed and watched the approaching rebels very closely. They walked with their weapons like they were book-bags and most of them looked like they weren't even old enough graduate high school much less soldiers in a war. Ofi greeted Bomi with a hug, and they spoke for a short while. Suddenly, he glared into the SUV more carefully until he met eyes with Sam, then walked towards us with Ofi following behind. Sam climbed out of the back of the SUV and shook Bomi's hand.

He was smiling very cordially and held his arms open in a hospitable gesture.

"Good news travels fast," Jon Bomi said. "I appreciate what you are doing for our people. Shall I call you Sam or Rapunzel?"

Sam and Ofi laughed, amazed that he had heard that story. "It means so much to me to be able to help."

"It's a pleasure to meet you," he continued, then took Sam's hand and kissed it.

"Bomi, Sam would like to meet the leader of G.R.A.D," Ofi said. "She believes in his cause and wants to make a donation as recompense for the crimes of her father."

Bomi's face went instantly from a warm smile to a dead poker face.

"Your father?"

"Mr. Raider has had his punishment, and it was terrible," said Ofi. "We do not need to speak of him anymore."

"I don't think you want to meet this man. You will not find him anyway. Everyone is looking for him, people who know this land much better than you, Ofi, or even me. The bounty on him is very high. You will not find him, of this I am sure." After a pause, he continued. "But he may find you, and that is not something you should look forward to."

Sam held out an envelope in her hand. Bomi took it slowly and looked inside at the money.

"Mr. Bomi," Sam said. "If you can get word to him without my team coming to any harm, I would be happy to give you that amount again."

"What do you have for Farrakhan?"

"Is that his name?" asked Sam.

"Like the man from the Million Man March?" puzzled Ofi.

"Of course, that is not his real name," Bomi replied. "Like the American Muslim leader, he is a gifted violinist, so he is called Farrakhan by some."

"Well, I don't know anything about the Million Man March," Sam quipped, "but you can tell him I have a million dollars for him, as well as something he might be even more interested in."

The man raised his eyebrows, looked at Sam, then looked at Ofi.

"The money is not here, Bomi," Ofi said, not actually knowing whether it was or not. "But I trust they can get it. They just spent a similar sum in Chad to begin that farm to give our people work and food. Samantha is sincere, if perhaps a little reckless."

"I have not met Farrakhan, but I know someone who has. I will talk to him," Bomi offered. "I believe you, Sam. You have given us something to make us hopeful, so I will try to help you."

Sam smiled and went to hug Bomi, who started to back off, but then accepted the embrace.

Sam never entered the Azize Refugee Camp again. Sergeant Nevers forbade it, because now that her presence was known, defending her in that setting would be too difficult. Not only did she respect his position, but she was far more interested in the development of RRO-one. The land she had purchased and her vision for it had taken hold of her. She wanted to be there to make sure the momentum was kept. If RRO-one were successful, it would be the foundation upon which to build something great for the people of Chad and Sudan and repay her family's debt to the refugees.

The team erected tents on the property and helped however they could as the farm began to take shape. Fink escorted Ofi back to the refugee camp, where she interviewed and hired additional men to speed up the work. She also had secret instructions from Nevers to favor deserters who might have military training. Nevers and Harris sourced rifles, which they began to train some of the men on, in case it became necessary to defend RRO-one.

This raised the eyebrows of the Conway people, but Sam assured them it was for security and in their best interests. This sort of precaution was not completely unheard of by Conway, and it was common knowledge that Chad faced internal stability risks and that neighboring Darfur was another destabilizing factor. Without a stronger reason to doubt Sam's motives, the construction company ignored the small-scale training and went about their business. Up went living quarters, a school, the agricultural buildings, irrigation, and farm-related and security fencing.

There were no signs of Farrakhan or G.R.A.D. until one day when Sam and her five guards were shopping at the fruit and food market. A man they did not recognized made eye contact with Nevers, then handed Sam a note before disappearing into the crowd. Back in the SUV, they found that the note contained an address in the neighboring town, Blue Nile.

For the first time, Sam's team seemed to be on high alert. They were all embarrassed someone had gotten so close to Sam and escaped. Concerned that the note might be designed to lure them into an ambush, they returned to the RRO camp to regroup. When they finally set out again towards Blue Nile, Lombard and Barnes were on motorcycles, one mile ahead of and one mile behind the SUV.

When they arrived at the address, they found a home with a seven foot wall around it and a large metal gate. A ten-year old boy came running from the side of the road and asked Barnes who they were. The boy had been told to expect Sam and he blew his whistle. The gates slowly crept open, allowing the entire team inside. Inside the compound, they looked around and saw that there were many rifles trained on them.

Impetuously and against Nevers's advice, Sam exited the car and began walking towards a man who was clearly there to greet them. Up until this point, she had believed that the man who wielded the machete against Gina and her father was the leader of G.R.A.D. But this was a different man. Something told her that this was the real leader. He lifted a microphone, and when he spoke into it, his voice was projected loudly through speakers. He told Lombard and Barnes to get into the S.U.V. and all of Sam's men to stay put there. In the van, Nevers started cursing himself. Why did we enter this compound?

"Please join me inside," said the leader of G.R.A.D. and walked into the house. When Sam strode in after him, Nevers opened his car door. He closed it again, though, after bullets strafed within two yards of the vehicle.

Now, the leader of G.R.A.D. and Sam were alone inside, and Sam was trembling with fear.

"Why are you looking for me, little girl?" he said. "Are you here to seek justice for your *Mami* and *Papi*? I am unarmed. Do what you came here to do."

Sam had not expected this. Strangely, it set her at ease.

"No. I am here to make things right right. This is bigger than me and you, Mr. Farrakhan."

"Don't call me that," he said. "Way too formal.

"What should I call you then?"

"Please, call me Aadil."

Sam slowly went into her bag and handed him the papers from her mother's safe deposit box.

Imam Aadil took them from her, and, after scrutinizing the second page, invited her to sit across a table from him.

"This is very good. Do you know what this is?" he said as he held the papers in up in front of him.

"I do. That's why I am here."

"If anyone knows you have these, you're a dead white girl," Aadil said. "Do not trust even your best friend with this information. There are some very powerful people on this list. Do you have any other copies?"

"Yes, but its back home," Sam said.

Aadil sat back on the chair and took a deep breath then threw his hand up, rejoicing at his fortune. Then, he leaned in to look at more of the papers. Sam waited patiently until he looked over at her. His eyes grew softer, and he took on a somber tone.

"I am amazed by you. It must have taken a lot for you to decide to give this to me. I must apologize for the death of your mother. I wasn't there, but I admit it was my representatives who did it. They are very angry and difficult to control."

"I have made my peace with you," Sam said. "We all have to answer to a higher power sooner or later."

"Yes, that is true," Imam Aadil said. "I have done a lot in the name of Justice for my people and will continue to do so. Allah will find favor with my actions or he will not."

At that point, Aadil turned the conversation to Sam's activities in Chad. She described her plans for the farm, and he expressed his respect for her. At that point, he invited Sam and her men to stay for dinner. Sam declined and told him she had to return to Ofi to help her with plans. Sam returned to her team that were happy about her safe return.

Sam's team left Aadil's compound at dusk and made their way back to the RRO camp. It had taken every bit of energy Sam had to walk in and face the

Imam. She placed her bag on Nevers's lap and laid her head on top of it. That was the first time she had shown any of her team one iota of vulnerability. The others took turns looking at her. She looked like a teenager, now. They were full of admiration and wonder at the bravery of this girl.

Suddenly, Nevers jerked Sam's head out of his lap. Sam wiped her eyes and looked through the window to see a large fire ahead on the road.

"This does not look good," Nevers said. Lombard is pulling over. Stop the truck!"

The first bullet came flying through the windshield hitting Fink, who had been driving the SUV, sending blood spattering into the back seat onto Nevers and Sam. The SUV rolled slowly to the side of the road.

"Cover me!" Nevers yelled. The others began firing as Nevers jumped from the back, opened the driver's side door, pulled Fink out, and took his place. The sound of multiple shots tearing through the body of the SUV sent everyone frantically cowering to the floor of the SUV. Nevers threw it into reverse and started to drive backwards slowly until Barnes jumped inside, then accelerated. Lombard was dead on the road. Nevers managed to turn the SUV around, almost turning it over on its side. The bullets kept coming until the back window was gone. Lombard and Barnes fired back through the window at the cars in pursuit. A pursuing cars hit one of the abandoned motorcycles and screeched to a halt, slowing down the others.

"We can make it out of here," Nevers said.

Sam remained cowering on the floor of the back seat after a loud explosion. The SUV lost speed after the engine stalled from being hit by a rocket

Sam heard the blades from a Black Hawk helicopter at the same time she saw Harris was dead. Nevers was beating his fist on the steering wheel. Sam saw that the situation was deteriorating and called Ms. Doyle on her phone to tell her predicament. Nevers looked at her and then straight ahead.

"Here I go." He took a deep breath, crossed himself, jumped out of the car, and ran around to reach through the broken back window for a grenade launcher. The helicopter had circled and was coming back towards the front of the SUV. Nevers walked out from behind, took one knee, and fired the grenade. A line of bullets came flying from the helicopter and ripped Nevers apart as the grenade from his launcher flew wide of the helicopter and exploded harmlessly into a hill. Nevers had bought Sam the time she needed to leave a message for Ms. Doyle explaining that the Sudanese government had sent their henchmen for her.

Sam and Barnes looked in each other's eyes, then walked out of the SUV with their hands up. The mercenaries from Lyceum executed Barnes without ceremony and loaded Sam into the helicopter. It was over.

I tried to control my emotions when Ms. Doyle broke the news in the house. Ms. Doyle had expected the worst–though she was upset, she had already accepted that Sam might not return. But this was my worst nightmare. I screamed and asked God why he would do that to me. Why do that to Sam, who had done so much good for others? Once again, I was left wondering why God gave me so much only to take it all away. Losing both Mamma and Sam was too high a price for my new life of privilege.

My life was fundamentally altered that day. I decided that day, no longer would I ask God for anything. But before I did, I made one final request. *God please take my life in exchange for Sam's safe return.*